Leon and Esther

An Historical Love Story

By Dorothy May Mercer

Recommended for mature readers.

REVIEWS: Here is what readers had to say about *Leon and Esther.*

5 Stars **Faith**

"While reading this book, I experienced a myriad of emotions, and this is what kept the pages turning. I fell in love with Leon, but not because he was described as muscled and handsome, but because of his ability to listen to his heart and obey what God had planned for him. When I read the first half of this book, I wished that more people could see that this life is bigger than us, that we all have choices we can make, and how we deal with those choices can determine our happiness, or demise. I loved the faith this family showed, and determination to stick together in an era where options for women in Esther's situation, were greatly limited, to the point where the reader has to remember, and can appreciate, how far the rights of women have come. The last half of this story, greatly pulled on my heart strings, I constantly had to put myself in Esther's shoes, and try to think like she would, being a woman of that time. I loved it, I loved being Esther, and loved being loved by Leon. With this said, I also loved the pace of the story, it moved along just as I like a story to, page turning. Five stars, because life isn't always easy, and this story demonstrates that with love, support, and a willingness to make the hard choices, can pay off in the long run." ...By Amazon Customer

5 Stars "Don't Let the Christian Label Deter You"

"This is a story of Esther, a young self-centered girl, who you really don't like at first, but then you watch her grow after something horrible happens to her, and to Leon, her knight in shining armor. Set in the 1900's, this novel gives you as real feel for the period in a small, rural farming community. You feel the pain and torment of the characters as they figure out how to deal with a situation no one should have to deal with. You laugh when they laugh, cry when they cry, and find yourself rooting for them to be able to make it work.

Yes, this is labeled a "Christian" novel, and the characters do seek guidance through prayer when times are really tough, but there is no Bible thumping nor will you be rolling your eyes, so yes it is a part of this story, but not the center. Do not let the label deter you. The book is well worth the read." ...By Paul Held III

5 stars **A Real Gem**

"I just finished reading the book *Leon and Esther* and I couldn't wait to post a review for other readers. It is a roller coaster ride of emotions, once I picked this book up, I just couldn't put it down. Dorothy [the author] magically places us in an earlier time where life is less about modern technology and more about the interpersonal relationships that surround us. Her book is set in the 1920's with themes of love, loss, tragedy and romance that are so basic to the human condition it is impossible not to empathize with the characters. Your blood will boil. Your heart will sing with joy as you are immersed into the lives of Leon and Esther. This book is definitely on my recommendation list." ...Elizabeth

More highly recommended books by this author:

"Stories I Haven't Told" From Barefoot Farm Girl to CEO in America, Memoirs of a Depression Baby

"Leon and Esther," An historical love story

The McBride Series, exciting mystery action novels, with a touch of romance.

"Car oo6 Responding" a good cop story.

"The Cocaine Chase" Cops versus Drug smugglers.

"The Immigrant and the Golden Coin," terrifying journey across Mexico and more McBride romances.

"The Cartel Wars," West Coast Cartel vs. McBride and friends.

"The Gang Bust," McBride destroys baby smuggling/political corruption and solves the Immigration crisis in a stirring ending. Juli and Mike wed.

The New Washington McBride Series, more action, suspense, with an exposure to human- trafficking cartels, plus human interest:

"The Fairfax Fix"

"The Arlington Alias

"The Savage Surrogate

The McBride Romantic Suspenses:

"Fran and Max," The Bungalow, a woman in hiding finds love

"Cynthia and Dan," Cyber War, terrorists threaten the White House

"Mary Beth and Sammy," Rolling Thunder, for young adults and up.

Coming Soon:

"Kelly and Tom," E.M.P. Armageddon, the worst nightmare.

ISBN 13: 978-0982718933

© Copyright 2011, 2013 by Mercer Publications & Ministries, Inc.

8651 Mohawk Ct.; Stanwood, Michigan USA 49346-9644

Dedicated to the memory of my parents, Leon and Esther, with love, devotion and admiration for all they survived and for the life they made for me.

The Author

Table of Contents

Author's Note:

Six of the main characters –Leon, Esther, Walter, Millie, Doris and Bill – in this story are loosely based on real historical people who lived during the time period. The family relationships, some of the basic facts and dates are correct according to my memory and research. The character of Leon is true to the type of man I knew.

The locations, for the most part, are real as are the times and settings.

However, the character of Otis and all the remaining bit characters are imaginary and have no relationship to any persons living or dead.

The personal stories and the dramatic events are <u>works of fiction</u> and are entirely my imagination.

The Author.

PROLOGUE – Esther and Otis

September 23, 1919

Esther sighed as she relaxed against the leather seats and turned her face into the sun. What a beautiful afternoon in Michigan! Fall was in the air. The sumac was already bright red. The green maple trees were painted with streaks of gold, red and orange. Esther closed her eyes and listened to the rhythmic clip-clop of the old chestnut-colored horse, Bess, as she pulled the buggy with ease.

Bess knew the way into town. She was a member of the family and had been pulling Esther into town for her voice lesson every Saturday for close to three years now. Besides, Otis had a firm grip on the reins. Nothing could go wrong. *Could it?* Esther adjusted her slender body in her seat. *Stop worrying and enjoy this day,* Esther admonished herself and sighed again.

Otis was the hired hand. He had shown up at the farm one day, looking for work. He would not or could not answer any questions about his family or from where he came. Father allowed Otis to stay in a small sparsely-furnished room in the barn while he made inquiries. Since no missing persons had been reported, Father filed reports with all the authorities and let Otis stay on until someone claimed him. Father could use another hand, and Otis was willing to live in the barn and work for his board and room plus a few dollars a month. Otis was what some people—in those days—might call "severely retarded" or "not quite right".

Otis was of medium height, had a stocky build and a rather ungainly gait from having one leg shorter than the other. His hair always seemed to need cutting. His nose was crooked from having

1

been broken sometime or other and he didn't bother to shave more than once a week or bathe, either.

The truth was Otis had come from a large family. His father had left home, and his mother was overwhelmed with her responsibilities. In his youth, Otis had suffered from the taunts of other children, so he never went far in school and was rather shy. At some point he was moved to an institution for the mentally handicapped and disturbed. One day he simply walked away. The place was so understaffed they did not notice him missing for several days and made little effort to find him.

Otis had a rather vague memory and little command of the language. He seldom said much. And when he did, one could barely hear and understand him.

Nevertheless, he followed orders and seemed content enough in his work. He was physically strong and such a great help to Father the family put up with him, so long as he stayed away from the main house.

Esther had given up trying to engage him in conversation months ago. If Esther spoke to him, Otis would look down at his toes, kind of shuffle his feet and mumble, "Guess I dunno, Miz Esther." Esther didn't know what to make of Otis. She was not entirely sure he could be trusted.

Esther led a happy carefree life with many friends and admirers. She was looking forward to her final year of high school. Next June she would be graduating and ready to go out and have fun.

I just hope I don't run into any of my friends today. What would they think if they saw me riding with this goofy moron?

Esther's thoughts drifted back to her argument with her mother just this morning. "But, Mother, you can't mean it. Are you serious? No way, no how, can I possibly ride into town with Otis."

"Yes, dear," said Mother, "Just this once. I really must have those few things from town and your Father needs Otis to pick up the feed from the mill. We're all out."

"But, can't we get by a few more days? You know I don't feel right about riding with him. What if someone sees us? Besides I can't stand him. I simply can't," she whined.

"Esther! Remember your manners!"

"Yes, Mother, I'm sorry," she said, but she didn't really mean it. "How about Doris? Can't Doris ride in with me?" Esther would not give up. She gave her long, silken brown hair a toss and frowned at her mother.

"No dear," said Millie. "I have some things for Doris to do here in the kitchen. Besides, Bill will be dropping by later to call on Doris. She needs to look her best for Bill."

"Oh good grief! It's always Bill. Sometimes I wish…"

"Esther Elizabeth! Enough, young lady!" Esther knew she had gone too far, when the middle name came out.

Millie rarely spoke harshly to her daughters. Calming herself, she softened her voice, "Your turn will come."

Esther turned away lest her mother see her start to blush. Matter of fact there was one young man she had her eye on; but so far he hadn't spoken to her privately. "I'll never act silly like Doris. Not for any man!" Esther declared with feeling.

"Mm," Millie shrugged as she turned back to her work, signaling an end to the conversation.

***

Otis pulled to a halt in front of Mrs. Lewis's house. "We're here, Miz Esther."

Esther opened her eyes, "Already? I must have dozed off".

Otis merely slanted a look her way with a sly smile, "Uh-huh," he slowly shook his head.

"Now, don't forget, Otis, you are to come back here and wait for me just as soon as you finish your errands." Esther slipped down the buggy and landed on her feet. Her hair gleamed in the as she swung around and skipped lightly up the walk.

Her voice lesson was one of her favorite times of the week. At age eighteen, innocent and beautiful, she had lots of favorite times and few worries. Her whole future beckoned ahead. *Soon*, she thought.

"Yes'm, I'll wait right here. I sure will Miz Esther." Otis slapped the reins once and Bess clopped forward.

***

To Esther's relief the horse and buggy was out in front when she emerged from Mrs. Lewis' music room. Esther skipped down the steps. She smiled and swung her lesson books into the seat before mounting-up herself.

Mrs. Lewis had praised her today, then again, she always had something good to say about Esther. Esther did well in all her studies, but it was still nice to hear.

Esther was feeling so good she even smiled at Otis. Otis gawked back at her.

Funny, I don't think I've ever noticed his eyes before. What an odd look! Otis was ogling her. "What are you looking at?" Esther demanded crossly.

"You," Otis answered.

Her face fell into a frown. "So? Why are you looking at me for?" Her brown eyes snapped.

"You l-look… purty." Otis's grin was almost a leer.

"Well, you stop it right now!" Esther climbed into the buggy and flounced into her seat. "You just turn this buggy around and take us straight home. Do you hear me?" She crossed her arms and stared straight ahead.

"Yes'm," Otis grinned as he gave Bess a little flick as a signal. "Yes… Esther."

"Humph," Esther huffed and tightened her arms. *I wish Doris had come with us. Darn her, anyway. Always mooning over her fiancé. 'Oh Bill. You are so strong and handsome.' Truly Bill isn't bad looking, but I will never act silly over a man.* Esther didn't need to.

Plenty of young men flocked around her like bees to honey without any encouragement. She was forever being teased, good naturedly, of course. They would laugh and call her "Short stuff." They might even pick up all ninety-five pounds and twirl her around until she screeched, "Put me down!"

In a way Esther was rather sorry they hadn't seen any of her friends, after all. Maybe she could have invited someone along, but probably everyone was home having supper. Her lesson had run a little later than usual.

Soon they passed the outskirts of town and Otis gave Bess a little more slack in the reins. A quick snap set Bess into motion.

This is good. The buggy is tooling right along. This way we should make it home before dark. Esther gave the sun an uncertain glance. It was edging closer to the horizon.

Just then Otis gave a hard pull on the left rein. Bess responded with a snort and a toss of her head. "Haw Bess, haw!" shouted Otis as he pulled even harder. The horse turned abruptly left as the buggy careened on one wheel.

"What are you doing?" screamed Esther. "You crazy fool! Are you trying to get us killed?"

Otis answered with another hard slap of the reins. "Giddy-yap, Bess, giddy-yap!" he shouted. Bess plunged through the ditch and into a rough lane.

Immediately the trees and brush closed around them, shutting out most of the sun's remaining rays and slapping Esther in the face. The buggy bounced and scraped. Bess was covered with sweat. The poor horse galloped ahead heedless of potholes and ruts. The buggy swayed dangerously.

Esther's heart was pounding. Her eyes grew huge, reflecting the terror she felt. *Mother of God! What can I do?* She couldn't jump out at this speed. But, if she didn't jump soon, they could topple over at any moment.

"Otis, NO!" she screamed and grabbed for the reins. "Pull back, pull back!"

Otis turned to look at Esther with mouth agape.

"Help me, you IDIOT! Help me stop this thing!" Esther gasped for breath as she pulled with all her might. Otis reached one strong arm across her and snatched the reins out of her hand. Esther fell back. Otis grabbed for her arm as she threatened to tumble out of the buggy.

"Whoa," he called. "Whoa back, Bess, whoa back," Otis commanded. Bess slowed almost as suddenly as she had taken off. Otis skillfully guided her nose into a thicket. Bess began to munch on leaves and grass.

Otis calmly pulled the brake and wrapped the reins around it. He turned to Esther without a word and hauled her into his strong arms.

"Arrhk," she screamed, "What are you doing? Get us out of here, Otis, you fool!" Esther slapped at him and dove for the reins again.

Otis seized her. She tried to jerk away. He muffled her terrorized screams with a crushing kiss. Her hands pushed against his chest to no effect. Then he smothered her face to his chest. Without a word, he reached behind the seat for a length of rope. He wasted no motion, skillfully tying her hands behind her back and a bandana over her mouth.

Esther realized there was no use screaming when no one could hear her. She pleaded with her eyes and mumbled into the cloth. Otis went about his work, grim-faced and determined. He laid her down on the seat and threw up her skirts.

"Nooommm!" she screamed, and thrashed, uncontrollably, back and forth.

Otis drew back his arm and slammed a fist into her head. She kicked out at him. Teeth clenched, he hit her in the chest, harder this time. She tried to twist away as he beat her repeatedly. She averted her head to protect her face. He slapped her hard with one hand as he wrapped his other hand around her throat, holding her down. He slugged her in the stomach and bile rose in her mouth. She started

6

choking. She stilled as she gagged on her own vomit. *Dear God,* she pleaded, *Help me!* Another fist landed in her groin.

Esther was weakening. The world was going dark around her. Esther became motionless. She sagged back, half on and off the seat. Her eyes fluttered closed. Her body expelled a long sigh as her head flopped to one side.

Otis watched her intently. Otis's chest heaved. He adjusted Esther's limp body. His jaw was firmly set as he held her roughly with the one hand and fondled her body with the other. He unbuttoned his trousers and let his member spring free.

It was over in seconds. Otis bellowed in triumph, held her tight, tensed with all his might and emptied himself into her.

***

It was total darkness as old Bess faithfully walked home, tiredly drawing the rig up near the barn. Otis leaped down and began unhitching the animal. He led Bess away toward the barn to put her into her stall.

Esther had not stirred, though her chest moved ever so slowly. Now and then her eyelids twitched. Silent tears rolled down her face. Numbness in her limbs gradually faded as pain and sheer terror took its place. Esther fought against reality as it demanded to return. Every muscle in her body screamed in agony.

Esther rolled and fell onto the ground in a quivering bundle. She laid there, chest heaving, for long minutes trying to still herself. Gradually she managed to pull up onto her hands and knees. Dimly she realized her peril wasn't over. She needed to reach safety.

Somehow she managed to stumble toward the house. She stood outside the kitchen door watching Millie as she busied herself in the kitchen. Esther waited for a few minutes after her mother blew out the lamps and headed toward the bedroom before she pulled open the door and hastened toward the stairs leading up to her own bedroom.

Esther threw herself onto her bed and buried her face between two pillows. Sobs racked her body. It seemed like an eternity before her body stopped its shaking and Esther was able to crawl under the covers. She had no energy to clean herself. Esther lay awake for hours alternately weeping and planning how she would hide this from everyone. Finally she fell into a disturbed sleep.

In the morning Esther hid the torn clothes and examined her bruises. Fortunately her face wasn't touched. She thought *I must hide these rope burns on my wrists.* She pulled on her favorite long sleeved flannel night shirt. This will work, but how can I stay in bed and avoid *questions?* She decided to feign cramps from her monthly flow in order to escape going to church.

As soon as everyone left, Esther threw a coat over her nightgown, grabbed one of Father's shotguns and hurried to the barn to confront Otis.

"Otis," she called. "Otis!" she yelled. "Come out of there, now!"

Esther banged on his door. "I know you're in there Otis. Open the door." She backed away with the gun raised.

"Otis, you come out of there right now, or I'm coming in," she warned.

The door slowly opened. Otis stood in the doorway looking down at his shoes. "H-hello, Miz Esther," he mumbled and swung his arms in embarrassment. He hid a slight grin and waited.

"Otis, look up," commanded Esther. "See this shotgun, Otis?" Holding the gun about waist high, she jabbed the gun at him and took a half step forward.

He raised his eyes just enough to peek at the gun.

"Otis, listen to me. You listen to me good!" Esther demanded.

Otis seemed to be shaking. He shrank away and crossed his arms over his body to protect himself.

"Don't move!" commanded Esther.

Otis flinched.

"You stay away from me, Otis. Do you hear me? Stay away from me and Doris and Mother. And you stay away from all the girls in town. It's wrong to touch a girl unless she says it is okay."

Otis quaked in silence.

"Otis, what you did to me was wrong. Wrong! Do you hear?" she screeched. The gun was shaking now. Esther tightened her grip and used the gun for emphasis.

"You stay here in the barn. You help Father, and never, never, NEVER COME NEAR ME AGAIN!" Esther screamed at him as tears began to flow. "I will shoot you with this gun. I will tell Father what you did and he will kill you, too. I mean it, Otis. NEVER AGAIN! You stay away from me or we will both kill you! First we will beat you up and then we will kill you!"

Otis backed away. He slammed the door and ran for the far wall. He cowered in a corner and covered his head with his arms.

Esther lowered the gun. She squared her shoulders, backed away and then turned and ran for the house. Esther returned Father's gun to its storage place.

Tomorrow would be a school day. All she had to do was to get up late and hurry out of the house to escape her mother's discerning eyes.

***

Leon and Esther

PART ONE

CHAPTER ONE – Millie and Walter

Two months later

Millie reached for the teapot and tiredly began to pour. "Walter..." she began.

"Mm, yes?" Walter raised his eyes from the book he was reading. He looked at her in inquiry.

Millie idly stirred her tea, gathering her thoughts.

Walter, a tall, rugged farmer with a wind-tanned complexion, sighed and set his book aside. "You needed to say something?" he asked as he reached for the oil lamp and turned it down a bit. "Millie?" he prompted again and gazed at her.

Millie drew a deep breath, "I think something may be wrong."

"Wrong?" Walter waited patiently. He struck a match to relight his pipe. Walter drew a few puffs and let out a stream of smoke.

It was evening and the couple was enjoying a few quiet minutes together after a long arduous day. Esther was in her room and Doris was out with Bill.

Walter eyed Millie with concern. Life was good. They had worked hard, increasing their farm in prosperity. Their two girls were almost raised. Doris would be married soon to a prosperous farmer whom they both approved. It was their younger daughter who caused the worried frown on Millie's brow.

"Well, uh...," Millie lowered her voice. "Have you noticed Esther acting strangely?"

Walther puffed thoughtfully. "Um, not really. What are you saying?"

"Well… it's nothing I can put my finger on. It's just, you know, little things."

"Hmm?" Walter met her eyes, "Maybe you'd better tell me what you've noticed." He knew his wife. She would tell him when she was good and ready.

Millie hesitated, "I know how you feel about Esther; but she just hasn't been herself. She used to laugh a lot and hurry from here in a rush of energy every morning, but now she is so serious. When she is supposed to be studying, I catch her gazing out the window with the book lying open in her lap. When she doesn't know I'm watching, she will sit for twenty minutes without turning a page, without moving."

"You really are worried about her, aren't you? Have you talked to her about it?"

"Well, I've tried," Millie sighed, "but she just brushes me off with some excuse. I've not heard her practicing her singing lessons in weeks. She used to always sing and hum around the house. I approached Esther's voice teacher about her at church last Sunday, but she hadn't noticed anything. I don't know what to think. Esther isn't eating like she used to, either. She brings half her lunch bag home, uneaten, and dawdles with her food at supper time. She refuses breakfast."

"She sounds love-sick to me. Appetite is the first thing to go," offered Walter, his grey-blue eyes twinkling.

"Don't make light of this, Walter."

"I'm sorry, Darling. You're right. I'll talk to her tomorrow." He set his pipe down and reached for his book.

"I've decided to speak to Doris about her," continued Millie, "if you don't mind."

"Excellent idea, Millie. You go right ahead." Walter tongued his pipe and bent to his reading. "We'll get to the bottom of this, Millie. Now, I want you to try to quit worrying. I'll wager it is just some teen-age phase she's going through. The same thing happened with Doris, remember?" He turned a page.

12

Millie rose and crossed the room to the stove. She picked up the poker and idly moved the coals around until they sprang into life. She added another log, returned to her rocker and picked up her mending.

Walter followed her with his eyes as she bent over the stove. *She's even more beautiful than when I married her,* he thought. *I'm a lucky fellow.* Soon he yawned and stretched his long, lanky body. "I think I'll go on in to bed," he said. "It's been a long day. You will be coming soon, I hope." He paused and looked directly at Millie, a knowing twinkle in his eye.

Millie chose to pretend she didn't see or hear. "I think I will wait up for Doris."

"As you wish, my dear. Don't stay up too long." Walter planted a firm kiss on her and left with good-natured resignation. They had always had a lusty relationship. He knew Millie wouldn't keep him waiting more than another day. Walter quietly closed the bedroom door.

Millie heard their bed give under his weight. It wouldn't take him long to drift off. *Walter has always been a good man and life-partner*, she thought. After nearly thirty years together, they understood each other quite well with merely a look or sigh. Few words were necessary.

***

CHAPTER TWO – Doris

The outside door rattled a bit; then with a kick in just the right spot, it sprang open and Doris breezed into the room, her cheeks flushed. Millie could hear Bill's buggy pulling out of the drive.

"Hi, Mother, I'm home," Doris's voice sang out.

"Shh, not so loud. Everyone's asleep but me," Millie cautioned.

"Oh, sorry," Doris answered in a stage whisper. She tiptoed across the kitchen to hang up her jacket.

"Come and sit with me a minute, Honey," Millie invited. "Pull up a chair over by the fire."

"Sure, Mom," Doris began, "Bill and I had the most marvelous time tonight. He took me on over to where we are going to build our house and we got out and walked all around where our kitchen is going to be and the dining room and bedrooms. It is going to be beautiful and so exciting! I can hardly wait. Don't you agree, Mother?" Doris bubbled with so much excitement her voice began rising again.

Millie lowered her voice and touched one finger to her lips. "Oh, Darling, I'm sure it will be. I'm so happy for you, and Bill, too. But I have something else on my mind I want to talk to you about."

Doris was even more beautiful than her sister, several inches taller than Esther, with an erect stature which added to her dignified, queenly appearance. Being in love had certainly added a rosy glow to her complexion, as well.

Doris moved to pull up a chair and sat near her mother. She turned her attention to Millie. "Of course, Mother, what is it?"

"I don't know quite how to say this," Millie began, "but I'm concerned about Esther. Maybe it's just my overworked imagination, but I was wondering…have you noticed anything about your sister? Any change in her behavior, anything unusual? Do you know if something is bothering her?"

Doris paused, as if in thought. "I guess I haven't thought about it, Mother. Is there anything in particular?"

"She seems so serious lately, just not herself, you know?"

"Well, I see what you mean. She has been kind of quiet. She's still a teenager you know. Moody."

"Perhaps… I suppose, but, she turned eighteen as of July. Isn't it about time she grew up?"

"Perhaps, but you've said yourself, everyone grows at their own pace," Doris countered. "Do you think she is feeling sad because I am going to be getting married? We've always been close. Maybe she is worried I'll not come to see her."

"There's a thought, but, I don't know…it still seems like something more."

"Maybe I just need to give her a bit more attention to reassure her. Try not to worry, Mother."

"Well, perhaps, but I'm a mother. I can't help but worry about her lack of appetite. She doesn't eat enough to keep a bird alive."

"Aha!" exclaimed Doris. "She's dieting again, which explains her lack of energy, too."

"Just the same, I wish you would keep your eye out."

Doris gave her a reassuring pat, "Leave it to me, Mother. I'll ferret it out of her, I promise. Is there anything else now, or can I call it a day?"

"Go on up, Dearest, and get your beauty sleep. You're beautiful already, of course. Here, give me a kiss good night."

"Goodnight Mother get some rest." Doris kissed her on the cheek.

Millie stroked her elder daughter's soft brown curls, "Goodnight Doris." She smiled. "Sleep well."

***

CHAPTER THREE – Esther and Doris

The Saturday after Thanksgiving, 1919

"Wake up, sleepyhead," Doris called out, her morning voice full of cheer. She bumped open the bedroom door with one hip as she carefully balanced a food tray laden with a hearty farm breakfast.

Doris set the tray on a bedside table and plopped down on the edge of the bed next to a motionless lump. "Wake up, Esther, and face the day!" Doris placed one hand on the lump and began to gently shake.

"Go away," groaned the lump as she pulled the covers over her head.

Doris moved to the window and raised the shade, "Look at this beautiful morning!" she crowed. "Look at the glorious sunshine!"

Back on the bed, Doris resumed her shaking, "Wake up, lazy-bones."

"Go away." Esther slapped at her hand.

"Come on, Esther, the food is getting cold." Doris poured a half cup of coffee from the pot. "Here, Esther. Have a sip of this, Honey, you'll feel better." Doris pulled the covers down from Esther's face.

Esther rolled over and cautiously opened one eye. "Mmmf," she moaned. She rose up on one elbow and peered at the food tray.

Doris quickly propped a pillow behind Esther's head. "How about a sip, now?" She held the cup forward. Esther took the cup in one hand and bent her head forward for a sip. She set the cup down on the tray.

"What are you doing up so early?" Esther inquired.

"Mother thought we ought to have a sisters' party. For old times' sake, you know."

"She must want something," mused Esther.

"No, I think she just knows we are running out of Saturdays together."

"Maybe she is working on us. Santa's coming soon, you know."

"Maybe she is." Doris poured herself a cup of coffee and lifted one of the plates toward Esther. Esther took the plate and placed it on the bed. Doris took the remaining plate and began to eat with gusto, washing down the food with coffee. "No one can cook like Mother. This is so delicious. Try some," she offered between bites.

"I'm not very hungry," said Esther, lifting one piece of toast and nibbling on the corner.

"Are you feeling all right?" Doris eyed her sister.

Esther leaped out of bed. "Gotta go!" Esther hurried toward the closet.

Doris followed her with her eyes. *What do I hear? It sounds as if Esther is retching. What on earth?* "Esther? Are you all right? Esther?" Doris hurried to the closet. "Oh, my dear, you're sick! Here let me help you."

Back in her bed, looking pale, Esther leaned back against several pillows. "I'm sorry," she managed.

"Just lie still. I'll take the tray. I'll get Mother."

"No, no, don't get Mother," Esther gasped.

"Why not? You're sick!"

"No, please don't get Mother."

"Well…all right…but why not?"

Esther just shook her head and sagged back looking wan.

Doris picked up the tray. "I'll be back," she promised.

Minutes later Doris returned, sat on the bed and crossed her arms. "All right, little sister… give!"

Esther merely looked more miserable.

"I want to know what is going on and I'm not leaving until I find out!"

Esther offered, "Nothing's going on. I just haven't felt very hungry lately."

"Not hungry, huh? Since when does not being hungry cause you to throw up after one bite of toast? Explain, Esther!"

"I only threw up once," Esther whined.

Doris eyed her suspiciously, pondered for a moment, gasped, and then asked, "How long since you had your last monthly flow?"

"I don't know. I don't keep track."

"How long?" Doris demanded.

"I've never been very regular." Esther rolled over and looked away.

"How…long?" Doris took Esther's shoulder and pulled her over.

"Just a few weeks." Esther couldn't meet her eyes.

"Look at me, Esther Elizabeth, look me in the eyes and say it again!"

Esther's eyes slowly lifted to meet her sister's. She blinked once as tears began to form. One began to slide slowly down her cheek.

"Oh, no! Oh, Esther," Doris whispered. She gathered Esther into her arms. "Oh, Honey, you poor thing. I'm so sorry. I can't believe this." Quietly she rocked to and fro and patted Esther soothingly.

Esther's tears flowed in earnest.

"Go ahead, Honey, cry it out."

The sobbing continued for several minutes. Finally Esther sniffed and wiped her eyes and nose on her nightgown. She leaned back once more. "Thank you, Doris. I'm sorry. I must look a mess."

"Honey, who did this to you?"

Esther looked away.

"Was it one of your boy-friends? Which one? Were you willing?"

Esther merely shook her head.

"Oh my Heavens, you weren't willing? Who was it? Daddy will kill him."

"Now you understand why I can't tell you. No one would believe me, anyway. It's always the woman's fault." Esther snorted and

18

started to tear up again. She grabbed a handkerchief off the night stand and blew noisily.

"Whoever it was, he forced you, didn't he?"

Esther nodded vigorously and blew again.

"Did he hurt you?"

"Yes."

"Badly?"

Esther nodded again. "I thought he was going to kill me. He almost did. I must have been unconscious for a long time, an hour, maybe. I don't know."

"Were you awake when he was, you know, doing it?"

"Well, not really. He had hit me so many times I just passed out."

"Well…then…how did you know? I mean how did you know what happened? How were you so sure he, you know, did it to you?"

"Well when I woke up my dress was all torn and muddy and my pantaloons were gone. There was all this blood and sticky stuff in my, you know, this area." She gestured between her legs. "I was so sore down there it hurt to walk for days. I don't know…I just assumed it was what he planned to do. I was still awake when he was hitting me and barely conscious when he ripped my dress."

Doris gasped and touched her mouth. "Go on, Esther."

"Well, I-I saw it, you know, his thing. He was holding it and hitting me and hitting me before I completely passed out. He had me tied up and I was choking on the cloth he had tied around my mouth. I fought and kicked him just as hard as I could. But, finally everything went b-black."

Esther began to sob again. Doris held her and stroked her for a long time. At length Doris whispered, "We have to tell Mama. She'll know what to do."

"No, no, please. You can't! You can't tell anybody, not even Bill. You can't! Promise me," Esther wailed and cried harder.

Doris sighed. *Dear God. What a mess!* She leaned her head against Esther's tousled hair and bit her lip. *What a mess!* Gently Doris eased her sister back against the pillows and drew the blanket up under her chin. "Go back to sleep, now, Esther. We've got plenty of time to figure this out, later." Esther sighed and closed her eyes. Doris quietly pulled the shades and stole from the room, closing the door behind her.

CHAPTER FOUR – The Same Morning

In the Farm Kitchen

"Mother, Father, I have something to tell you."

"Oh?" they chorused.

"Yes, Doris, what is it?" Father spoke for them both.

"You aren't going to like what I have to tell you." Doris looked sadly from one dear face to the other. How she hated to speak these words, knowing their hearts would be broken, especially Father's. Esther was the apple of his eye. She knew he loved them both, more than life, but Esther was his baby.

Mother spoke up, "Well, if you're going to tell us something, tell us!"

"I'll get to it in a minute," said Doris, "But, first, I need to say something. You can't imagine how sorry I am to have to tell you this; and, if I could possibly spare you this information…I would give anything…"

Walter stared at her intently. "What is it, Doris?"

"Also, I want you to know I must break a confidence to tell you this." Doris gathered her courage. She drew a deep breath. "It's about Esther."

"Esther! Oh my dear, what is it?" Millie looked at Walter in dismay.

"Well, I found out what's been wrong with Esther. She told me just this morning."

A feeling of dread descended over the room.

"You have to promise me you won't be angry. Promise me?"

Millie nodded. Doris looked at Walter. "Father?"

"I can only promise…" Walter could barely choke the words out, "…I will try, but… you can't expect the impossible."

"Okay, just try, because it's not her fault. It really isn't. You've got to believe me," Doris pleaded.

Two pairs of eyes bore into hers. No one breathed. "Well, the thing is Esther has missed a few periods and…" Doris hesitated, "And she threw up this morning without eating a thing."

Millie gasped and covered her mouth. Walter abruptly leaped to his feet. "You don't mean…?"

Doris nodded, "Yes, Father, we think so. We're pretty sure."

Millie was incredulous. She stared at her hands folded on the table. She seemed to be speaking to herself. "My own daughter…of course." Millie slowly shook her head. "She's with child." Millie bit her lip. "All this time, I should have known." She looked at Walter, helplessly, tears threatening to spill. "How could I have been so blind?"

First Walter paled, then clenched his fists and colored beet red. He turned on his heel and stalked out the door without a word. Doris moved to follow.

"No, let him be," advised her mother. "He will need some time alone, the poor man." Millie shook her head sadly, sighed and moved to draw water into the teakettle. She poked up the fire and set the teakettle over it. Then she sat down at the table and rested her head on her hands.

Doris sat quietly, eyes downcast, waiting for her mother. At last Millie raised her head and gazed at Doris. "Who is the father?"

"She wouldn't tell me," answered Doris. "I have no idea."

"Why are you so sure it wasn't one of her boyfriends?"

"Esther told me she was forced," said Doris.

"Oh, dear Lord, my poor baby!" wailed Doris. "Does she know who did it?"

"Yes, I think she does," said Doris, "but she won't tell on him."

"Why not? She must have some reason."

"Because I said Daddy would kill him and she thinks she needs to protect Daddy."

"Oh… well…you may have a point there. I don't know what Walter would do. He is a peace-loving man, but this is different. He's her father."

"I agree with you, Mother. We can't put him in the position of having to decide."

"Did she say anything more? Think, Doris, think."

"Well, Esther said he hit her several times and tied her up."

"What else?" prodded Millie.

"Um, well," Doris hesitated. She didn't want to tell Millie about every detail. "I don't know if this means anything but she mentioned he wore coveralls."

"I see," said Millie thoughtfully. "Did you get any impression about how long ago this happened?"

"No, I didn't, but it can't be very long ago. Remember the Sunday she stayed home from church with her monthly flow? It has to be since then. She can't be very far along."

"Yes, I remember. She had gone into town the day before, for her voice lesson."

"I was out with Bill."

"Well, I guess we will just have to pray hard and wait and see what happens next. Thank you, Doris. I know this has been difficult for you. You felt as if you were betraying your sister. Not all decisions are easy, but you did the right thing. Esther needs her whole family now. Go get some rest, Honey. Walter should be back soon and then we'll all talk."

***

CHAPTER FIVE – The Family

Later.

Millie, Doris and Walter sat in the living room talking quietly together. They looked up when they heard footsteps descending the stairs. Esther entered the room looking rather disheveled. She paused with downcast eyes. Walter cleared his throat and hesitated. Millie opened her arms wide, "Come here, Baby." Soon the entire family joined in a group hug.

Millie spoke first, "You poor darling. Let us share your sorrow. We are your family and we love you, no matter what." The others nodded in agreement. Esther sniffed.

Walter blinked back a few tears and cleared his throat, "You are not alone any more, Esther. At a time like this we all need to stick together."

"We will help you through this," Millie added.

"B-but, Mother what can I do?" Esther held back her tears.

"Well, no decision has been made except we all need to sit down together, talk this over and make some decisions." Millie took Esther's hand and led her over to one of the four chairs which were drawn up in a circle. "Here, now, please sit down, Esther." Millie gestured for the rest of the family to join them.

Esther's shoulders slumped. Her eyes were downcast in shame. Millie and Doris turned in unison toward Father. Walter cleared his throat and began, "Esther, we have been talking it over while you were napping."

Esther sighed and wiped her nose.

Walter continued, "Esther we think we need to pray for guidance in this situation. Do you agree?"

Esther nodded and sniffed.

"All right, Esther, here's what we'll do. In a minute we are going to all join hands with you and pray together for guidance and healing.

24

Tomorrow, we will go to church together. Maybe the service will give us some insights. We'll see, Esther. Are you in agreement with us?"

Esther nodded, "Yes, Father, Mother. Thank you."

Everyone reflected in silence for a long minute. Doris spoke, "Sister, dear, we love you. You know, don't you?"

"L-love you, too," stuttered Esther, "and I'm sorry…so sorry."

One by one they rose and reached out to one another. Hands joined they bowed their heads. Giving voice to the plea on each heart, Walter began, "Lord, we need your help…"

***

CHAPTER SIX – Leon

Church school was finished and it was time for the break before the worship service began. Leon had led the Young Adults class. He was pleased with the discussion for the day. Since today was the first day of the Advent Season the topic was appropriate for his group.

They discussed the reaction of Joseph to the discovery Mary was pregnant by the Holy Spirit. *Speaking of Spirit, the class had a spirited discussion–pun intended.* Leon smiled to himself at his private joke.

Several of the single men had teased, voicing their opinions on one side. "Nonsense, no way should he wed with a wh…oops I mean sullied woman," while the ladies blushed and huffed delicately, "Joseph should stick by his betrothed."

Several of the young men had recently returned from the war in Europe and were actively seeking wives. It made for playful interaction between the sexes.

Folks were milling around and visiting as they waited for the worship service to begin. Leon could overhear the discussion continuing around him with good-natured humor. The men enjoyed baiting the ladies. Leon was glad he had sparked an interesting class discussion today.

He always spent a great deal of time in preparation and even more time in prayer. It paid off in the large and faithful number of students he had in his class. Leon had been leading the class ever since he recovered from near death during the influenza epidemic a year ago. He had not forgotten his promise to God.

Leon was a tall, fit, handsome and eligible bachelor at the age of thirty. He had no shortage of secret female admirers. He seemed to have eyes for the lovely Winifred, who was also in his church school class. Recently Leon had been seen escorting her to several social functions. Leon worked hard as manager of a local farm and played hard when off duty. He was admired for his horsemanship and joined

26

in with the other young bucks in racing contests and sporting events. None of this took his eyes off his promise to serve God, even though he wasn't quite certain what it would be.

Today's sermon picked up on the Advent theme. After a challenging sermon, the congregation waited in silence and meditation as they were called up row by row to partake in Holy Communion.

As he watched the communicants moving by, Leon reflected on what he had taught and heard this day, especially on Mary's plight and Joseph's commitment. Leon tried to open himself to God's leading, praying God would lead him in whatever way he should go, the same way God had led Joseph and many other Biblical characters.

Leon's eye was caught by the family moving across in his peripheral vision. He knew the parents well and admired the two girls, of course. Both were beautiful, but neither one was for him. Doris, the elder was already engaged to be married and Esther, the younger, was too young, a mere eighteen, still in school. Besides she was short, a full twelve inches shorter than he. Leon could probably pick her up with one arm, and span her waist with his two hands.

Something about Esther drew his eye. Leon watched her steadily as she knelt. Yet, when the elements were offered to her, she looked down and kept her hands prayerfully folded. *Was it possible she refused the elements?* Leon watched her closely as she rose to leave and turned in his direction for a second. *It looks like tears. Can she be weeping?* The family moved into a nearby pew. Leon tried to watch without seeming to stare. *Yes, she is taking out a handkerchief and wiping her eyes. Walter is putting his arm around her. I believe she needs my prayers. Everyone has their troubles,* he thought. *You just never know what is going on in people's hearts.*

Leon closed his eyes and lifted up a simple prayer, "Oh Lord, Thou who heals all things and mends all hearts, I humbly lift Thy daughter, Esther, to you in prayer. I earnestly beg Thy forgiveness on her behalf for whatever is needed for her. Thou knowest her heart and her need.

Lord, if it be Thy will, use me as your messenger for Thy daughter, Esther. Or, if it be Thy will I not interfere, guide me, as well. I pray Thy Holy Spirit in helping me to discern Thy will. In the name of Thy precious son, our Lord and Savior, Jesus Christ, Amen."

It was not unlike other prayers Leon had offered for any number of his friends and students.

Leon waited quietly, eyes downcast, until it was his turn to go forward. With the others he knelt at the altar listening, thinking on Christ's sacrifice. As he closed his eyes, a glorious sense of light and warmth came over him. He felt alone in the presence of God, surrounded by the Holy Spirit and filled with an overpowering sense of love. It filled his heart and overflowed with tenderness toward Esther.

Leon remembered nothing else about the day other than he almost floated home. There was sense of rightness about what he should do. He must pay a call on Walter and discuss Esther's future. Perhaps he was being sent to comfort Walter.

Whatever was meant to be, Leon would be open to the Lord's leading.

***

CHAPTER SEVEN – Leon and Walter

Walter was in the barn loft forking down some hay for the horses when he heard a male voice calling his name. "Up here," he answered, "Up here in the haymow."

"I'm coming up," the voice called.

Walter stuck his fork into the hay and turned toward the ladder. "Who's calling me so early Monday morning?"

A familiar young man emerged, brushing off his body and picking a few stray stalks out of his thick brown hair. "Morning Walter," he greeted and held out his hand. "How are you this fine day?"

"Well, as I live and breathe; if it isn't the varmint who keeps beating all the young fellows around these parts, and a fine morning to you, too, Leon. What brings you out, today? Are you looking to buy one of my prize hogs, or rams, perhaps, to upgrade your miserable flock?" he teased. "Pull up some hay and sit a spell," he invited.

Leon lay back in the sweet-smelling alfalfa. "Well, Walter, thank you so much for your generous offer, but I'm not in the market to introduce inferior blood lines into my prize-winning flock. There *is* something of yours I have in mind, if you would be so obliged as to consider an offer."

"Perhaps I might consider something along those lines," replied Walter, "Although, I'm not in a selling mood, you understand." Walter was already gearing up for an enjoyable bargaining session with one of his favorite young neighbors.

Sunlight peeked through the cracks between the barn siding and fell on Leon's countenance. He squinted thoughtfully at the dust motes drifting in the rays. "Well, Walter, I have an eye on one of your daughters." He hesitated for a moment, chewing on a stalk of hay, and realized he had been holding his breath. "It's the correct thing to speak with her father, first. I'd like to call on her, with your permission, of course."

Leon waited nervously. A long moment passed, before Walter spoke. "Young man, I appreciate your coming to me first. I believe I can," he cleared his throat, "spare you some embarrassment. I'm sure she has no idea of your, uh, feelings for her. I have nothing but admiration for you, Leon. You are an ambitious young man and would make a fine son-in-law, but you obviously don't realize the situation, although it escapes me how you could have failed to notice." Clearly, Walter was trying to let the young man down gently.

Leon felt a bit puzzled. *What on earth is Walter talking about?*

"Leon, apparently you are unaware my daughter is in love and is already promised to another man. The marriage will take place in seven month's time. I'm sorry Leon, but I can't encourage you toward my daughter. She and Bill are planning their home already."

Leon sat bolt upright, his mouth agape. Slowly he shook his head and tried to speak. "N-n-no... not Doris. I know about Doris and Bill."

"Then, who?" Walter propped up on one elbow, "Who are you talking about? You can't mean Esther!"

Leon looked away and spoke quietly, "Yes, I mean Esther." He was chagrined. "I'm asking you for permission to call on Esther, your younger daughter."

"Oh," Walter sagged back into the hay and looked away. Memories returned with a vengeance along with despair. "Oh...you meant Esther...my little girl, Esther."

Leon was confused. "What is wrong, Walter? Does it make any difference which daughter? I know she is young, but we have lots of time. I'm willing to wait, you know, take it slow. Give her time to grow up."

Walter sighed, "Yes, it might make a difference, Leon. It's just well...there may be some things you don't know about Esther."

30

"I don't understand…what things?"

"Just… things. I really can't speak about it now."

"I'll wait." Leon settled back in the hay and crossed his arms.

"I don't think you understand me, Leon. I can't speak about it for some months, maybe never."

"Then, I'll just wait." Leon crossed his arms tighter.

"Leon, please, I can't say any more. I would really appreciate it if you would not speak about this to anyone."

"You have my word. I will speak to no one except God."

"You talk to God? You seem to be a fine Christian, Leon, but you talk to God, huh?"

Leon hesitated. *Well, I might as well roll the dice. Here goes…*"Walter, would it surprise you if I said I pray to God and sometimes, he answers me?"

"God answers you?"

"Not as thunder coming out of the sky, but in a still small voice deep inside. Perhaps it is just a feeling, an assurance something is right. If there is a question I'm struggling with I can pray to God for guidance."

"I see," said Walter, "Go on."

"When I was so sick last year, I almost died, you know. Edith made the trip down to take care of me. My sister, Edith, you know, the nurse?"

"Yes. Go on." Walter's voice carried no clue as to what he was thinking.

Dear God, I wish I knew what he is thinking. Oh, well, in for an inch, in for a mile. "There were times when I was delirious. Edith never left my bedside. I truly believe she saved my life," said Leon. "Later Edith told me I talked and mumbled a lot in my delirium. She said I seemed to be praying. What she didn't know was how I was bargaining with God. I promised to serve him if he would save my life. And if it was my fate to die, I prayed he would take me to heaven."

"I see," mused Walter. "Go on, please."

"After I recovered, I remembered my promise. It seemed as if God was close, trying to guide me. After I experimented a bit, I kind of drifted into a way of praying which seemed to help me. I started out with small decisions asking God to help me chose, then searching for his answer. I learned if there were too many choices, prayers didn't help at all. But, if I could narrow it down to two choices and present them to God one at a time, I would sense a positive feeling towards one and negative feeling toward the other."

"Mm…feelings, it's all this is…just feelings?" Walter sounded skeptical.

Leon had no answer. Doubting was easy. Faith was hard. *I guess Walter is either going to believe or he isn't.*

"I take it you are trying to convince me God gave you a 'feeling' you should call on Esther? Humph!"

"Yes, I'm sure of it. After sleeping on it I feel more certain today."

At length Walter spoke, "I appreciate your frankness, Leon. I believe you are sincere; but I need to be sure, too. I need to think about this, maybe do a bit of praying, myself." He rose up and looked directly at Leon again. "Let's both pray about this for a few days. Then if you still feel as you do, we'll talk again, if you agree, Leon?"

"Yes it's a perfect suggestion, Walter. Our minds need to be in accord on this or else it isn't from God." Leon jumped up and stuck out his hand. "Let's shake on it," he offered.

Walter took his hand in a firm grip. "Goodbye, Leon, I will see you soon. Let's give it three days."

"Three days," Leon nodded. "Goodbye, Walter." Leon shimmied down the hay chute and was gone.

    ***

CHAPTER EIGHT – Dreams

Later in the evening, Leon knelt beside his bed. "You heard Walter, Lord. I pray you will guide him as you have done for me. I pray you will confirm or deny my feeling whether or not I should court Esther. Send me a dream, Lord. In Christ's name I pray. Amen."

He laid his tired body on the bed, fell asleep almost immediately and began to dream.

***

In the dream Leon is standing under some kind of bower. The flowers brush the top of his tall head. He looks down at a petite girl standing beside him. She is dressed in a beautiful white gown. *Is this a ceremony?* She is holding out her trembling hand to him as he slips a slim golden band on her finger. *Must be this is a wedding ceremony.* "You may now kiss the bride," intones a voice. Leon steps toward the dainty girl and almost has to lift her off the floor to kiss her. Even so, she fits perfectly in his arms. Leon releases her and strains to identify the girl.

Suddenly they are fleeing in a hail of rice. Leon feels elated.

***

Next morning Leon awoke with the dream fresh in his mind. What does it mean, Father? No answer. Well, I have two more days to think about it. I trust you will let me know. Thank you for the dream, Lord.

***

Walter barely knew what to make of the astonishing visit this morning. He went about his chores, all the while turning the meeting over and over in his mind.

Was Leon's coming here the answer to our family prayer? Does God pay such attention to petty human affairs? It was clear Leon felt God was leading him to call on Esther. But, one call does not a marriage make. Such a marriage would certainly solve our dilemma, but what about the child? Leon is a virile young man in the prime of life. Would he take on the burden of another man's child? Well, he doesn't have to know, does he? If we hurry the wedding date, as soon as possible, it could all be accomplished before Esther starts to show.

Good heavens, what am I thinking? Get Thee behind me, Satan! I'm not about to stain my soul and everyone else's with such a deception. No, there has to be another way out of this mess. Should I send her away to one of those homes for unwed mothers? Walter's heart felt heavy at the thought of Esther all alone in some unfamiliar city, giving birth without her mother and sister to help her.

No, I just don't feel right about it. There I go feeling again. Maybe there is something to this 'feelings' thing, though I doubt it. Too simple. Too unreliable. I'm a practical man, not a dreamer.

I've heard the men in town talking about someplace down in Ohio where girls go to get rid of their unwanted pregnancies. Maybe I could discretely inquire. But, O God such a possibility gives me the shudders. Yeah, I hear you, Lord, feelings again. Ok, so what do you want me to do about this situation?

Does Leon have the answer? Was Leon's visit from you? Suddenly the sun came out from behind a cloud and bathed the earth. Walter looked around in some astonishment. Maybe so, maybe so, he thought. I don't understand it, but I admit I feel better now.

   ***

Walter didn't think about it again until he and Millie were lying in bed at night, talking over their days. "I had a visit from Leon this morning."

"Oh I wondered when I saw his horse tied up by the barn. Did he want something?"

"It was the strangest visit," he said. "You may not believe this, but he wants to call on Esther."

"I'm surprised. What about Winifred? I thought he was sweet on her."

"He didn't mention Winifred."

"Well, what did you tell him?"

"He and I are going to think about it for a few days, maybe do a little praying, too."

"Ah, I see. Well, I guess it is okay if it is God's will," she declared with more trust than Walter had. "Goodnight, dear." She rolled over and went to sleep, leaving Walter to worry, alone, far into the night.

There was one other tormented family member under the same roof. Esther's troubled heart had her alternately staring at the ceiling or wrestling with the covers and spinning in her sleep. There was no question in her mind whether she had been 'leading Otis on.' Quite the contrary, the man gave her the creeps.

What was a modern girl supposed to do, hide herself under a burkha? It's so unfair! I refuse to feel guilty! Then she felt guilty and started to cry again. Damn him, damn Otis the creep! Look what he has done to me. I'm ruined! None of the boys will have me now. I might as well be dead!

She pounded the pillow into shape and flopped down again. Esther's tears ran until she fell asleep. In her dreams her mind replayed the rape scene over and over until she woke up, again, sweating and shaking. *Oh God, oh God. Why me?* She moaned and pounded the pillow again. *Oh God, what's to become of me?*

Again Esther fell asleep. This time she dreamed of her parents weeping beside her casket.

   ***

In her dream somehow Esther's body is lying dead in a casket while she is also standing off to one side. She turns to someone standing beside her. "What happened? Do you know?"

"Oh, yes, didn't you hear? She died giving birth to the baby? So sad."

"Oh, I see. Her parents seem so grief-stricken."

"Yes, they have taken it pretty hard. The baby didn't live either, two tragedies in one. Of course, the whole town knows she deserved it. Her parents were too good to her, spoiled her, you know."

***

Esther's cry woke her up. The dream seemed so clear to her. How selfish of me to think only of myself! My dear parents must be suffering. They had such high hopes for me and I have let them down, completely. How disappointed they must be! Esther spent the rest of the night reflecting on how precious her parents were to her, how they loved her and sacrificed everything for their daughters.

Before dawn her mind was made up. She would move out east with an aunt. When the baby came she would either care for it or put it up for adoption. This scandal must never touch the rest of her family.

A sense of peace settled on Esther's heart and she fell into a relaxed sleep.

***

CHAPTER NINE–Bad News

"Have a seat, Leon," invited Walter as he spread fresh straw for the sheep. "Be with you in just a second."

Leon pulled up a nearby barrel, sat watching Walter and chewing on a straw. "Mighty fine-looking pen of sheep you have there, Walter."

"Thank you kindly, Leon. You have excellent judgment," chuckled Walter as he pulled up a stool. "I suppose you are here to talk about Esther."

"Yes, I am, Sir. Have you come to any conclusions?"

"I might return the same question to you, Leon. After thinking it over have you changed your mind?" Walter asked, hopefully.

"No Sir, I haven't. I have thought and prayed about it and feel even more confirmed in my decision. I would like to court Esther and, in time, offer for her hand, if she will have me, which remains to be seen, of course."

"Oh, she'll have you, I've no doubt. In a way I was hoping you might change your mind. It might have saved me from having to break some bad news to you."

"Bad news?" Leon's heart sank. Bewildered, he looked at Walter and waited for an explanation.

"I'm hoping you followed my advice and spoke to no one about this?"

"No one, but God," Leon replied. "I gave you my word."

"Very good," said Walter. "Then, I need your further word you will not reveal what I am about to tell you to anyone so long as you live no matter how you feel about it. I must have your further word before I can continue."

"You have my word, same as before. I will speak about it to no one but God."

"All right," Walter sighed in resignation. "It hurts me to tell you this, more than I can say. Esther will not be a fit wife for you, my son. Esther has been shamed…ruined."

Leon was stunned. "What? What do you mean?"

"My daughter, Esther…Esther is with child! With child, Leon."

Leon stood up, shocked into silence.

"I'm so sorry, Son, I wish it weren't true. Dear God, how I wish it weren't true! You will keep your word, won't you? You won't mention this? Before you run off, promise me."

Leon shook his head and sat back down with his head in his hands. "It can't be. Dear God, I was so sure."

"Will you keep your word?"

"Yes, of course, don't worry. But Walter, I'm so astounded! This was the last thing I would have thought. She'll be marrying the father, of course."

"Well, actually we don't know. She refuses to name the father."

"What! Surely you will insist."

"So far I have no choice. She is afraid I will kill him and well I might. She doesn't want me to be a murderer."

"You're no murderer, Walter. But surely you can insist on a marriage."

"She says the man forced her."

"Oh."

"She says she hates him. She can't stand him."

"I see. Well, I guess I see. No, I don't see, really."

"Doris doesn't know who it was, either, but Doris confirms Esther's story. Apparently the man beat her badly and nearly killed her."

"God in Heaven, how horrible!"

"It wasn't one of her usual boyfriends in town, at church or school. So, it must have been someone we don't know, perhaps a stranger."

"Do you know what you're going to do?"

"Well, there are a few alternatives, but we haven't decided yet. We agree it will be a family decision."

"Yes, it should be a family decision. I agree with you. Well, Walter, you and your family have my deepest concern and sympathy in this time of trial. I do not know what God has in mind, but I will keep praying for all of you."

"Thank you, Leon, you are a good man. I would have been proud to have had you as a son-in-law. I'm sorry.

"Goodbye for now, Walter." Leon held out his hand.

Walter took his hand. "Goodbye for now, friend."

***

CHAPTER TEN – Decisions

Leon mounted his prize-winning horse, Gibraltar, and left with mixed feelings, concern for Esther and her family yet pondering God's directions for him. Somehow he didn't feel God was finished with him. *I need to simply stay focused on the Lord and carry on with my life trusting God would reveal those things to me that God wants me to know.*

Leon knew it wasn't always necessary to understand God's mind. Sometimes God meant for people to proceed on trust, only lighting the way one step at a time.

On the way home, Leon replayed the events leading up to this day in the biblical sense. As he did, more teachings were revealed in his mind.

Am I living the modern-day version of Joseph? What are you teaching me, Lord? Is Esther my Mary?

There are always parallels to human problems to be found in the teachings in the Bible. I can draw from those teachings to help me in my quest. And yet, I must take care not to push the comparison too far. There are similarities with Joseph and Mary, but many differences, as well.

For one, neither Esther nor I are saints. We are human. Is God simply using these biblical examples to instruct me? It doesn't necessarily mean I should make the same decision Joseph made. I still need to seek God's guidance in my personal situation, as well as the guidance of Godly advisors and my own God-given intellect.

Soon Leon was back home and submerged in all the details he had been neglecting. It was good to stay busy with ordinary things, grooming his horse, feeding the animals, caring for the sick or injured lambs, preparing orders, instructing the hired hands, conferring with the boss. His bed was a welcome thing. Leon said his prayers and was immediately asleep.

***

Next morning Esther came down the stairs for breakfast feeling hungrier than she had in weeks. Her mind was made up. It felt so good to get the decision behind her.

"Good morning, Esther."

"Good morning, Mother. Beautiful morning isn't it?"

"You are acting chipper this morning. Are you feeling better?"

"Yes, I am hungry for your special apple pancakes and maple syrup. What d'ya say? Got any pancakes over there?"

"It will be my pleasure. I'll have it ready in a jiffy. So, please sit down, Esther. I'll pour you a cup of coffee and you can tell me how you slept. Did you have a good night?"

"Well, yes and no." Esther stirred a spoonful of sugar into her coffee and added a dollop of cream. "I dreamed a lot, Mother. I was wakeful part of the night thinking. The important thing is I have reached a decision. I know what I'm going to do about this baby."

"How so?" Millie ladled three blobs of batter onto the sizzling grill and added a few apple slices. She fetched a plate, slipped it into the warming oven over the stove and set the pitcher of maple syrup on the back of the stove. "Would you mind fetching yourself some silverware and set out the butter, please, Esther?"

Esther moved to gather those things, sat back down and sipped her coffee. "I've decided to move back East, Mother, to live with Aunt Lily. Remember what she said when she visited, 'Come and see me sometime? The door is always open?'"

"Um, well, maybe."

"Well, she said it and so I'm going to write her today before the mail goes out."

"What about your schooling, Esther? Surely you've thought it through."

"I'll stay until the end of the semester. I think I can make it through until then without showing too much. Afterward I'll have to

41

leave. They wouldn't allow me to stay. I'm disappointed I can't graduate with my class, but school policy won't allow pregnant women."

"Maybe they would allow you if you were married, Esther. You know your father would force that horrible man to make your baby legitimate, if you would only speak his name."

"Married women aren't allowed either."

"Are you sure?" Millie reached the warm plate down from the warming oven.

"I'm not going to marry him, he's a stupid horrible man. I'm sorry, Mother, but you just have to understand, it's impossible."

"I hope you know what you're doing, child."

"I'm only doing the best I can. I'm doing what I think is right. Aunt Lily will have me, won't she?"

Millie slipped the pancakes onto the plate. "No problem there, Honey, and she'll love it, I'm sure. We'll miss you so much, Esther." Millie set the steaming plate of pancakes in front of her daughter and caressed Esther's head with her hand.

Esther bowed her head for a silent prayer, buttered the pancakes and poured a smile on each one with maple syrup before she drowned them with enough syrup to melt the butter.

"Do you think Father will help me with money for transportation?" Esther bit into a dripping forkful.

Millie poured herself a cup of coffee and sat down at the table with Esther. "Of course he will, darling, and with an allowance for your needs, as well. Don't worry about it. Not one bit."

"Thank you, Mother. After the baby comes, I will try to finish my schooling and look for work. I can't go on being a burden to you and Father."

"You are not a burden. You are our daughter, the joy of our lives."

"Not such a joy lately."

"Maybe, but we love you dearly, no matter what. No one escapes life without experiencing some sorrow."

"Will you speak to Father about my decision, or shall I break the news?" asked Esther.

"Well, let me think a minute." She took another sip of coffee. "Let's see… if we can get Doris and Walter together and tell them at the same time it might be best. But, we'll play it by ear. Make sense?"

"Makes sense." Esther sopped up the remaining syrup and savored the last bite.

"All right. Now I have some things I need to do. Would you like to clean up the dishes for me?"

"Sure, Mother go ahead. I'll finish up here. Let's see if there is any more coffee over there." They exchanged kisses on the check before Millie left the room.

As she wiped off the table, Esther began composing a letter to Aunt Lily in her mind.

***

Leon managed to rise each morning before the sun was up and before the morning's duties began. He aimed to spend at least one hour in study, prayer and meditation. Each day he sought out scripture to aid in his meditation– scriptures about people who struggled with decisions or those who were seeking guidance.

One day it was the story of Samuel as a boy whom God was calling. Another day it was the story of the prophet, Gideon, who put out a fleece and asked for a sign from God. *Should I put out a fleece? No, I don't think so. I should not doubt God when He has already shown me what to do. God does not give new directions until you follow the last one He gave you.*

One doesn't put out a fleece lightly, either. It must be a serious matter which can't be settled any other way.

As the days progressed Leon's conviction grew stronger and his doubt fainter. After three mornings of study, meditation and prayer,

Leon knew what he had to do. He had to offer for Esther. This was what God required of him. Leon trusted God would not lead him directly into a mistake. It had to be the best for them both. Leon believed, in time, God would fill their hearts with love for each other. After all, the Bible says God is Love and Leon believed this.

Leon's mother had taught him to love God right from the cradle. Leon was the youngest of six children. He had an elder brother who had grown up and left home before Leon was born. The others were sisters. Leon's father and mother were parted when he was just a babe. As a consequence he was raised in a female household.

Although finances were almost non-existent, Leon's mother was a God-fearing woman who had a profound influence on Leon's life. He loved his mother very much, even though she could give him very little by way of material goods or education. Leon was forced to drop out of school by the ninth grade to go to work.

Later when he was old enough to leave home, Leon moved from Milbank, South Dakota, to Michigan to take a position with the Hubbard's. After he had apprenticed with them for six months, he had done so well they made him farm manager. He remained there ever since, bringing the farm into prosperity with modern methods, hard work and good management. Leon was careful with his money and had saved half enough to buy his own farm. It would take a few more years to realize his dream. Good farms didn't come cheap.

He dreamed of having a wife and raising a family of his own along with sheep, cattle, hogs and his favorites, horses and chickens. He also planned a variety of crops. He knew about crop rotation and building up the soil. Everything they needed could be raised on his dream farm. Ideally, it would have a good 200 acres of tillable soil, two or three fenced pastures for the horses and sheep and another pasture for the cows. There should be abundant water resources and a mature woodlot.

Leon could easily picture Esther as his helpmate. She was little, but she came from good stock, as did he. This pregnancy was a bit of a problem, but they could handle it together. He would raise the child as his own. They would plan for a large family. This child would merely give them a head start. Maybe it would be a son to grow up and help Leon with the farm, or, maybe a daughter to help Esther when the babies came along. Leon knew he couldn't rush Esther into having another child right away.

Leon was experienced. He knew how to please a woman and he knew how to space the babies out. He would give her time to grow up and adjust to being a wife and mother before allowing their second child. Leon was a patient man and she was young. They would have plenty of time to have the rest of their family. Oh, yes, indeed, Leon's mind was made up. He would call on Esther this weekend. But first he had to see Walter.

    ***

CHAPTER ELEVEN – Pals

"Morning, Walter."

"As I live and breathe. Didn't we just end our business three days ago, Leon? I declare, you keep turning up like a bad penny. You are always welcome, of course."

"How ya' doin', Walter?"

"Actually, I'm doin' pretty darned good, since you asked."

"I mean how are things, you know?" Leon shuffled uncomfortably.

"Well, things have a way of working out, don't they? Doesn't pay to worry too much," he added, mysteriously.

Feeling impatient, Leon retorted, "All right, Dodes, do I have to drag it out of you. Stop looking like the cat that swallowed the canary and answer the question!"

"Now, see here, young man. It will do you well to show a little more respect."

"You are right. Beg your pardon. I have no right to ask … well... uh… I guess I'd best be shoving off."

"Not at all. Come into my office, Leon. We'll share a cuppa something and enjoy a bit more privacy than out here in the barnyard."

Walter's farm office was little more than a closet in one corner of the horse barn. It was equipped with shelves for books on horse breeding, agriculture and money matters. A wooden desk held a lamp, a ledger, pen and inkwell, and various papers scattered around.

Walter reached behind a bookshelf and drew out a small bottle filled with amber liquid. "I keep this for special occasions and medicinal purposes, of course," he chuckled. "Will you join me?"

"Since it's you, just a half-shot, if you please."

"Here you go, pal. Wet your whistle." Walter clicked Leon's glass in salute and took a sip. "Here's to the women in our lives."

Unaccustomed to hard liquor, Leon sipped cautiously.

"Now," said Walter, "It's really quite simple. My darling daughter has taken us both off the hook. She has written to her Aunt Lily, Millie's half-sister, back in Connecticut. We expect to hear back in a week or so. But, there is no question Lily will be more than pleased to have her."

Leon's gut sank. "Connecticut?"

"Right you are. Good ole' Connecticut. Esther's leaving right after final exams, in mid December. Hopefully she will get out before the worst of the winter storms."

"Esther's traveling all the way to Connecticut by herself? Alone?"

"Yep," Walter chuckled and took another healthy sip.

"You're not worried about what might happen to her?"

"Nope." Walter thought better of it. "Well, maybe just a little, but she'll be all right. She'll do fine, I'm sure of it. Esther can handle herself. She is a grown woman, after all."

"Just who are you trying to convince?" accused Leon.

Walter turned in his chair and gazed out the window at nothing. "You weren't fooled, were you, son? Truth is I'm worried sick." He turned back and set his cup down on the desk with a note of resignation. "I shouldn't be drinking this stuff, it doesn't help." Walter blinked and seemed to shrivel.

Leon capped the bottle and set it back on the book shelf. He stacked the cups and put them aside. He gripped Walter firmly on the shoulder. "Walter, I think I have a better plan. I came here to tell you about it and get your approval. Will you listen?"

Walter nodded, "All right, go ahead and tell me. Somehow, I don't think I'll like this."

"All I ask is for you to keep an open mind and hear me out. Will you do it?"

Walter nodded, leaned back in his chair and reached for his handkerchief, preparing to have a good blow.

"Here's the thing, Walter, I've been thinking and praying for three days now. Nothing has changed my mind and I feel even more strongly about it. God has convinced me Esther and I are meant for each other.

"I have plans, Walter. I can provide for her if you can help us out just a little. I've saved about half enough for a good-sized farm for myself and a family. I'm hoping I can either put a down payment or lease some property and get started. I'm strong and healthy, Walter. I've learned a lot about running a farm profitably. I think I can do it, I know I can do it, Walter.

"I won't rush her into having a whole bunch of kids in the first few years. We'll have this one and then we'll wait a decent length of time before I burden her with another one, maybe three, four, even five years between babies. She's young, Walter, but I have a lot of patience and I can teach her while she grows up.

"I hope you will say yes, Walter, but I can't wait too long. I have to convince her to marry me before the middle of December. What do you say, Walter?"

Leon waited while Walter thought it through. At last he raised his head and spoke firmly. "Well," Walter cleared his throat, "I respect your sincerity. You could be right. I haven't felt good about this Connecticut thing all along; but I just didn't have a better solution to offer."

Walter paused to light his pipe. "You don't have to sell me on your ability to provide for Esther. God knows you are the best farmer in these parts and the best horseman, too."

Walter puffed on his pipe in between using it to gesture for emphasis. "No question but we will help you. I can give you brood stock and chickens to get started, a team of work horses, and loan of

48

equipment. Millie can stock up Esther's pantry with her canning. She always makes enough for an army. You buy a farm nearby and we'll be proud to get you started."

Walter was getting more excited over the plan. "Esther would be a fool to turn you down, Leon. But I must say, son, you've got your work cut out for you. Best you get started convincin'." Walter rose and thrust out his hand to Leon.

Leon choked a bit and grasped the hand firmly. "Thank you, Walter. Wish me luck."

Walter pulled him forward in a big bear hug. "I wish you all the luck in the world. God go with you, son." Walter broke out a big smile and heaved a sigh of relief.

"I know He will. Good bye for now, Walter. I'll be back on Saturday to call on Esther, say about three in the afternoon." Leon took his leave, whistling.

***

CHAPTER TWELVE – Leon Comes Calling

Saturday arrived with a rush of activity. Millie had been up since dawn baking and decorating little cakes and cookies for tea. As soon as the girls finished breakfast, Millie set them to work dusting and cleaning the house from top to bottom, airing out the parlor and polishing the cherry tables. All the doilies were hung out in the sun to freshen up. Esther fetched the silver tea service down from the attic and the girls giggled and fussed over it, polishing it within an inch of its life. Soon they could see reflections in all the pieces. Crystal candle-holders were washed and polished dry. China cups and saucers and little plates were cleaned as well. Pretty linen napkins were washed and pressed.

Millie had carefully saved all these fine things since her wedding. Some were handed down from mother to daughter. Some had come from the old country. As they worked, Esther and Doris plied her with questions about each piece.

It had taken some time for the girls to select Esther's gown for the occasion. It was a high-waisted blue silk, which gathered and fell from just under the bust-line in soft folds, the final complements being a hand-woven lace collar and three-quarter length puff sleeves. Esther was too petite for a large formal ball gown with multiple petticoats. This gown was slender in the latest style and fell just to her calves. Esther would wear pantaloons and a chemise underneath, long stockings and tiny size 4 ½ slippers in matching blue.

During all the hubbub, Walter had been banished to the barn. "Take the dogs and cats with you and shut them in," insisted Millie. Walter was only too glad to leave, muttering about all this fuss being a waste of good time.

***

Saturday morning seemed to drag by for Leon. He had informed his employer he was taking the afternoon off. He planned to wear his usual Sunday outfit of suit, tie and white shirt. He had only one and it was already pressed and hanging in his wardrobe.

Part of the terms of his employment provided for the maids in the house to do his laundry, sewing, mending and preparing of his clothes. If necessary, Leon could have done any of these tasks himself, he had been a bachelor long enough, but according to his employer his time was too valuable for such pursuits thank goodness. He vowed he would never let on to his future wife he was handy with the needle. He chuckled and imagined Esther in their living room, sitting in front of the fire one evening, bent over her sewing.

Oh, yes, he had been thinking about Esther a lot lately. How would it feel to hold her small body close to his? When he had held Winifred, she came up to his chin. *I must take Esther dancing and find out.*

Leon spent the morning doing a few chores and idly preparing his horse and buggy for the trip. He groomed his horse with long brush strokes, carefully easing the snarls and burrs out of the mane and tail and fixing them in a fancy braid. *Is this a little too much? Maybe I'll leave out the ribbons.*

He polished the silver buckles on the harness, trimmed and polished the hooves and checked the feet for pebbles and cuts. His stallion, Gibraltar, seemed to sense the excitement, prancing and moving about more than usual. Leon quieted him with an apple and stroked his nose. "There you are. You are a beautiful beast, for sure."

Leon talked to all his animals, especially his horses and even the chickens knew his gentle voice and would come running when they heard it, squawking and flapping their wings.

Leon checked the clock in the barn office for the umpteenth time. It had scarcely moved since the last time he checked.

***

Doris turned away from the window, "It's him! He's coming, Esther."

Esther rushed to the window. "Oh, how handsome he looks!" Both girls watched intently. "See how the horse sparkles and gleams in the sunlight, his coat so black and sleek! Look at him prancing. Leon drives so skillfully! I can't believe how lucky I am. How do I look, Doris?"

Esther had been standing ever since she donned her dress, lest she sit and cause wrinkles. Her silken hair shined with just the tiniest bit of oil Doris had brushed through it. They had spent an hour at the kitchen stove while Doris patiently heated the curling irons.

Esther was not blessed with curly hair like Doris, but Doris had accomplished a flattering "do" on it, nonetheless. Esther's hair now hung in one long graceful curl almost to her waist. Tiny wisps escaped along her face and forehead, just enough to frame and soften her face. The sides were discreetly pulled back from her face and fastened in the back with a blue bow trailing long ribbons.

"You couldn't look lovelier, sister-o-mine. Now, hurry upstairs before he knocks on the door. You may use a dab of my best perfume behind each ear and on your wrists. Wait until we call you before you come down. It would not do to seem too eager, would it?" Doris gave her a peck on the check. "Here's one for luck. Now hurry."

Esther tripped lightly up the stairs.

Walter was in a hearty mood. A rap came on the door and Walter opened it with a smile. "Come in, come in, Leon. Esther is expecting you. Millie and Doris will see you to the parlor and I will call up the stairway to see if Esther is ready."

Leon greeted the ladies with a polite half-bow and removed his hat. "Good day, ladies, you are looking beautiful as always."

"Good day, Leon, come this way, will you?" Millie said, motioning Leon to a place on the settee. She and Doris took the remaining two seats. "I trust you had a pleasant ride over. The trees are so barren this time of year."

Leon carefully placed his hat on his knee and leaned back in the uncomfortable piece of furniture. It certainly wasn't made for his lean and long frame. "Yes, indeed, ma'am, the horse moved right along. I'm afraid I'm a bit early."

"Not at all, not at all. Esther will be down directly."

Doris rose and offered her hand, "May I take your hat, sir? I will take care of it, then run up and see what is delaying my sister."

"Thank you, so very kind of you." Leon offered his hat.

Doris hurried up the stairs where Esther was waiting breathlessly. She had overheard every word. Doris giggled, "He looks so handsome, Esther! You are going to have to try not to swoon, I declare."

"Is it time to come down, now?" asked Esther.

"Almost time. Just give me one minute to get Mother and clear out of the parlor. Then you can make your entrance." Doris turned and flew down the first half of the stairs, then slowed to a dignified pace. Entering the parlor, she signaled for her mother to leave. "Esther will be down shortly, Mr. Douglas."

"Thank you, Miss Dodes, but call me Leon, please."

"Certainly, Leon, and call me Doris." She smiled and backed toward the door.

Millie rose. "If you will excuse us Leon, Doris and I will get the tea things ready."

"Of course, ma'am." Leon rose and bowed slightly before resuming his seat.

Leon was not without nerves. *Should I stand or sit?* Before he could make up his mind he heard footsteps on the stairs. A vision of beauty glided into the room and stood before him. Leon looked up into her brown eyes, dumbstruck. Suddenly realizing he was still seated in the presence of a lady, he hastened to his feet. He stood gazing at her for a long moment. Speechless, he bent and lifted her hand to his lips.

Esther found her voice first. "Good afternoon, sir. So kind of you to call."

Leon gestured toward the settee and they both sank down grinning at each other. He was still holding on to her hand. "Yes, indeed," he said. "I took the afternoon off from work." *What a dumb thing to say. Come on, now, Leon, you can do better. Where is your silver tongue?* "You are looking lovely today, Esther." *Good try, a little better. Keep going. Don't forget to smile.* Leon smiled at her.

Esther withdrew her hand. "Thank you, kind sir."

"Have you been well, ma'am?" Leon asked. *Oh no! Dimwit. Don't ask about her health.*

Esther answered without notice. "Oh yes, I have been in the best of health."

Liar, thought Leon, *but what did I expect she'd say? 'Oh, Leon, I've been suffering terribly from morning sickness.'*

Leon searched for a safe topic. "How has school been for you this fall? Are you enjoying your classes? By the way, call me Leon and may I call you Esther?"

"Thank you, sir...er... Leon. Yes, I really enjoy my classes. It can get lonely here on the farm, sometimes."

"Ah, so you are a city girl. You enjoy your girlfriends and the boys, too, I suspect. No one as lovely as you can possibly be neglected for long."

"I enjoy my friends, of course, but I'm not just a city girl. I love the farm, really. I only said it can be lonely at times. Don't you feel the same way, too, occasionally?"

"Well, yes, I suppose you are right, although, I'm usually too busy to notice. Beside my animals are my friends."

"I see why you are so successful. We all need a balance, don't you agree, Leon?"

"Oh, indeed we do!" *Mercy, it sounds beautiful to hear my name on her lips.* "I hope you don't think I am being too forward, Esther, but I brought the buggy today in the hopes you might consent to go riding with me for a short distance."

"How kind of you, Leon! However, I think Mother and Doris are about to serve tea. It may be too close to dark by the time we are finished."

Dark, hmm, yes, perfect. "Let's wait and see what time it is when we finish. Perhaps then you will give me your answer."

Doris and Millie had been waiting for some signal. An antique tea cart had been brought down from the attic, tightened, touched up and polished. They began pushing the teacart from the kitchen to the parlor.

Esther sat primly on a stool, poured the tea and offered a selection of tiny cakes and cookies. Leon dwarfed the teacup in one large hand and held a lemon cookie in the other. He seemed to remember playing "house" with his sisters long ago, perched on a similar uncomfortable chair while his sisters served first him and then all their dolls.

Leon smiled at the memory and reflected to himself Easter wasn't much more than a grown-up doll, herself. He devoured the delicate cookie in one bite and helped himself to another. "These are delicious. Did you make them?" He brushed a few crumbs away.

"Why, yes, I helped. Doris and I worked together. Here, would you like another? How about a teacake this time? It is a special recipe."

"Yes, thank you." He ate the cake. "How scrumptious! I'd ask for your recipe, but I'm afraid I don't cook."

"Would you like to take some home with you? Mother can bundle up a sample of each, for you."

"Yes I would, thank you Esther."

"Would you like more tea?"

"No thank you. I've had enough. What do you think? Is there time for a ride?"

"Yes, I believe there is, if you are ready to go."

"I'm quite ready, Esther."

"All right. Just let me get my bonnet and shawl. We'll tell Mother we're leaving."

Esther was back in a flash carrying her shawl and Leon's hat. Leon took the hat and offered her his arm. She laid her dainty hand on it and led him out into the kitchen. "We'll be leaving now, Mother. Leon has offered to take me for a ride in his buggy."

"Will you be back for supper, Esther?"

Leon answered for her, "I had in mind we might stop in town for a bite at the restaurant. What do you say?" He looked from Esther to Millie.

Millie answered, "Your suggestion sounds like a wonderful plan. Please have her home by midnight, Leon."

"Oh, we'll be back well before midnight. I have early morning chores to do before leaving for church."

"Of course," Millie agreed, wiping her hands on her apron. "You two run along now and enjoy the rest of the afternoon."

Esther kissed Millie's cheek and whispered, "Thanks, Mother." She smiled at Leon as he held the door for her.

Esther modestly held onto her skirt as she attempted to mount up into the buggy. "I guess my legs are just a little bit too short for this step," she laughed.

"Not to worry, young lady. I came prepared for this," said Leon as he whipped out a step stool, set it into place and offered his hand.

"Why, thank you, kind sir. This is just what a lady needs."

"I think of everything," Leon chuckled modestly and boosted her up into the buggy. "And look at this," he said as he unfolded a handcrafted quilt from the back. "May I tuck you in?"

"This is so lovely. Did you make it yourself?" she teased.

"Yes, I whipped this up last evening and thought of you with every stitch," he boasted as he climbed on the other side of the buggy and smiled at her with a twinkle in his eye.

"Oh, go on! Who did you borrow this from… Mrs. Hubbard?"

"Oh dear me, I do believe you have found me out. I hope you don't mind if we share."

"Not at all, it would be so cozy, really." She offered him a corner of the quilt.

Leon moved closer and snuggled under the quilt. He lifted the reins and gave them a practiced twist with a soft, "Giddy-up" to his impatient horse. Soon they progressed slowly out the driveway and turned toward town. Leon shifted the ribbons into his left hand and offered his right to Esther with an inquiring look. She laid her dainty hand in his open palm. He closed his hand around hers and grinned.

His hand was so strong and warm. She felt completely safe in his company. "Do you sing?" she asked.

"Doesn't everyone?" he quipped.

"Some more than others I should say."

"Let's give it a try. I'll start one and then you can start one."

Leon began to sing to her in his full golden baritone, "Put on your old gray bonnet, with the blue ribbons on it, while I hitch old Dobbin to the sleigh." He grinned at her and motioned for her to take it away. Esther answered in her pure mezzo-soprano, "Through the fields of clover, we'll ride off to Dover, on our Golden Wedding Day." Then they laughingly sang it once through together.

"How splendid!" Esther exclaimed, "I had no idea you could sing so beautifully."

"Nor I, you. C'mon, now it's your turn to choose."

"Um, let's see if I can think of one which fits as well as your selection. How's this one? Pony boy, pony boy. Won't you be my Tony boy? Don't say no. Here we go. Off across the plains. Marry me. Carry me; Right away with you. Giddy up, giddy up, giddy up, Whoa! My pony boy."

Leon threw back his head and laughed. "How perfect! Let's do a duet," and they did.

"Your turn," said Esther. "Do you have another one?"

"How about another duet?"

"Sure, I'll start… Down by the old mill stream, where I first met you, with your eyes so blue… (Leon joined in) dressed in gingham too. And it was there I knew that you loved me, too. You were sixteen, my village queen, by the old mill stream."

"You are a wonderful singer," complimented Leon, "I'm impressed."

"Thank you so much, I love to sing."

"Oh, I do too. We have something in common, don't we? Well, Esther, here we are in town. Anyplace in particular you would like to go? Uptown or down?"

"You choose." Esther realized they had driven right by the horrible spot with the ghastly memories, where she had been raped. Leon had kept her so distracted and happy, she hadn't even noticed.

Leon was driving down the hill to the best restaurant in town, the one down by the riverside. He tied up the horse and escorted her inside where they were greeted by a smiling host. "Good evening, sir, Miss. We have our best table waiting for you, Mr. Douglas. Come this way, please." Leon held her chair for her. "Your waiter will be right with you."

The host bent over the table to pour ice water into each glass and light the candles. He reached over and pulled a bottle of champagne out of an ice bucket, popped the cork and offered a sample to Leon. He sniffed, sipped and nodded.

"Champagne for the lady?" asked the host.

"Just a half glass, please," said Esther.

"The same," said Leon. The host poured both servings and melted away. Esther was enchanted by the white linens, the soft music, the flickering candles, and the shiny black water reflecting spots of lantern light, with a pair of white swans gliding lazily by on the surface.

Leon gazed at her in silence, captivated

Esther turned to her escort. "This is divine, Leon. Thank you so much. I've never...ever... oh my, words escape me. Just thank you. I'm having a wonderful time."

Leon's eyes gleamed, reflecting the flames. Silently he raised his glass and gazed at her intently. "Here's to the most beautiful woman in the room," he said and took a sip.

Esther was a bit flustered and blushed prettily. She was saved from a reply by the approach of the waiter. He presented their appetizers with a flourish.

Leon nodded approval. "I took the liberty of ordering ahead, Esther. I hope you don't mind. Do you like the champagne?"

"I must confess I've never tried it before."

"You'd best try just a little. This champagne is perfectly legal, the alcohol content is too low to qualify as actual liquor. It is more of a sparkling grape juice of no harm to you at all. Enjoy it."

"I'm glad to hear it's safe. It tastes really good, would you fill my glass, please?"

"Michigan voted to prohibit alcoholic beverages in 1916. Let's see, you were only fifteen then. I don't suppose it meant much to you at the time."

"Not really," said Esther. "I haven't been following it very much, as Father never has spirits of any kind in the house. Perhaps you could explain it to me." She took a little sip and began on her appetizer.

Leon suppressed an outright smile, reflecting on Walter's secret supply stored in his barn office. He went on to tell her the history behind the Temperance movement, while they ate. "Of course, there were several Michigan counties which had gone dry before the statewide referendum passed, thirty-nine in all, I believe. They began popping up as early as 1907, when Van Buren County was the very first. You were just a little girl then."

"True," said Esther. "This is fascinating. How do you know so much about it Leon?"

"I suppose I just like to read a lot." He started in on his main course. "I'm sure you know with the passage of the eighteenth amendment to the Constitution, the entire country is going dry. It starts sometime after the first of the year, January sixteenth if I'm not mistaken. Leave it to Michigan to be the first state to outlaw alcoholic beverages."

"Really? I guess I didn't know. So, how is it working out?"

"I'm not sure if this is fit for your delicate ears," he teased, "but, there is no shortage of illegal booze coming in from Windsor and from Ohio. Ha-ha. It's said there is so much booze flowing into Detroit from Toledo on U.S. 25, the Dixie Highway in Monroe County has earned the nickname 'Avenue de Booze.'" He took a few bites while Esther laughed merrily.

"Hysterical name," Esther grabbed her water glass to keep from choking.

"Of course, our own Methodist church has been in the forefront of the Temperance movement. Liquor has ruined so many lives. I've seen it and lived it. My father had a problem with liquor."

"Oh, I'm sorry."

"Thank you, Esther. His experience is why I feel rather strongly about it myself. I wouldn't want it to be a habit in my family, er, I mean, in the family I hope to have someday."

Esther looked down and blushed. They bent to their eating and were quiet for a while. There was much left unsaid between them.

***

Leon kept the horse to a slow walk on the way home. Esther leaned back against the seat, humming softly to herself. The harvest moon was rising over the tree tops. She began humming "Harvest Moon" taking care not to sing the words – *a bit too explicit*, she thought. Leon considered the words and decided to whistle along, as well.

He reached for her hand. She offered it willingly and smiled up at him. He raised it to his cheek and then set both their hands down together atop the comforter. There was a lot more he would like to do with Miss Esther, but not on their first date. As he walked her to her door, he was sorely tempted to take her in his arms and kiss her lips, but restrained himself and settled for kissing her hand.

"Thank you for a lovely evening, Miss Esther," he said, gallantly.

"You are welcome, kind sir. I had a wonderful time."

"Shall we do this again, perhaps?"

"Perhaps," she teased.

"I was thinking about next Saturday. Would you care to join me for a picnic, weather permitting, of course?"

"Yes, I would," agreed Esther.

"Shall we say about eleven? I have a place in mind about one hour's ride away."

"Yes, at eleven. I'll be ready. Goodnight, Leon."

"Until Saturday, then. Goodnight Esther."

Doris was waiting at the head of the stairs. "Come into my room and tell me all about it."

"I'd rather you would come down the hall to my room," replied Esther. "You can listen while I get ready for bed."

"What was it like? Did he kiss you? Isn't he tall and handsome? Where did he take you?"

"Enough, already! Just hold your horses, lady! It was wonderful. No, he didn't kiss me, but we held hands and sang. The moon was just coming up and it was so romantic. I wish I didn't have to leave so soon."

"Yeah, I know. Tough luck, darn it. Maybe you can come back, you know, after the baby. You do plan on coming back, don't you? Of course you do."

"I don't know, Doris. People are going to suspect, aren't they? I may have to go someplace completely new and start over."

"Oh, please, don't! You can come and live with Bill and me. You know you will always be welcome."

"Oh, Doris, my dear sister." Esther paused, holding her dress. "You will always be my best friend." Esther hung up her dress, turned and began removing her stockings and undergarments. "The tea was just perfect. You and Mother outdid yourselves. Thank you so much."

"You and Leon made a handsome couple. You were cute and pretty, sitting there, pouring tea."

"I was shaking so badly, I thought I was going to spill it"

"Wasn't he funny, holding a dainty teacup in his big paw?"

"Wait 'till I tell you about the champagne," Esther giggled and slipped a nightgown over her head.

"Champagne! Ooo-la-la, Oh you kid!" Doris rolled her eyes and made little circles with her palms.

"Well, it wasn't real champagne, more like sparkling grape juice with just a smidgeon of alcohol so as to stay legal. But, it was delicious, and we drank the whole bottle. He asked me out again and I agreed."

"How exciting! How soon?"

"Not until next Saturday, a whole week away."

"We'll start planning your outfit tomorrow. Goodnight, Esther."

"Goodnight, doll-face."

***

CHAPTER THIRTEEN – The Picnic

It was unseasonably warm for the first of December, yet rather late in the season for a picnic. Leon had come prepared with warm bricks and extra quilts in the buggy. Esther didn't mind when he pulled her next to him and put a warm arm around her. Esther snuggled up against him and began to relax.

It had been another one of those hectic mornings, helping Mother with the morning chores and getting ready for her outing with Leon. It was exciting to think she actually had a beau. She was determined to put her pregnancy out of her mind and enjoy the day just as if everything was normal.

She and Leon found plenty of things to sing and chat about. The trip went quickly. Soon he pulled the buggy into a charming little park tucked into some sheltering pines. Several picnic tables had been turned over and secured for the winter.

"Come with me." Leon offered his arms to swing her down out of the buggy. "I'll show you around." He took her by the hand and led her off to explore the park. They had the place all to themselves. Together they walked over to the far side of the park. Esther tried to keep up with his long strides as they walked to a lovely little brook bordering the park. They found a place to sit and watched it gurgling over rocks and stones. Leon smiled at her, "You like?"

"It's so peaceful and beautiful here."

They sat quietly for a while, just enjoying. At length, Leon stood and offered his hand, "Come with me, madam. I will show you the dining room." He led her to a small log building she had previously overlooked. It was enclosed on three sides and open to the brook on the fourth side. In the center was a stone fire bowl already set with tinder, kindling and logs. Several comfortable chairs were arranged around the fire bowl. The place was lit by overhead skylights with an opening right in the center to allow the smoke to escape.

"Shall I start the fire?" asked Leon.

"Oh, please do. This place is magical! How did you ever find it?"

Leon bent to the fire. "Ah, I am acquainted with the owner. He is letting us borrow it for today. Rather nice, isn't it? It will be cozy warm in no time. Would you like to sit and watch the fire while I bring the picnic things over?"

"May I help?"

"Not this time, thank you. I have everything under control." He strode away.

Esther was left to gaze at the fire by herself for a few minutes. Strangely, she wasn't the least bit frightened while alone with this man.

"Ah, here we are, madam." Leon took a seat next to Esther and placed the picnic basket between them. "How is my fire doing?"

"It's blazing away quite well, don't you think?"

"Quite well, indeed!" He took a poker down from its hook and began rearranging the logs to suit. "There, good enough job. Now, let's see what's in this picnic basket. I'm starved. How about you?"

"Not starved, but I could eat. May I serve you?"

Leon sat and turned his hands into fists. "Here now, wench. Bring me my ale and wild boar," he roared.

Esther chose a linen napkin and tucked it under his chin. She poured some cold tea into a glass. "Your ale, sire." She handed him a plate with two sandwiches, an apple and a piece of cheese. "Your wild boar sandwiches, Your Majesty." She dropped a quick curtsey.

Leon pinched her cheek, "Ah, Me Pretty, be off now." He gestured. "Shall we meet again, later, eh?" He waggled his brows and twitched an imaginary mustache.

Esther dissolved into gales of laughter.

***

Leon and Esther walked hand in hand back to the buggy. He swung the picnic basket into the back and turned to face her with a smile. She looked up into his eyes and swayed in his direction. He placed his hands on her shoulders. "Esther, I…may I…um…" He grinned with some discomfiture… "Oh, hang it all, I'll just say it: I had such a good time today. Being with you, in this beautiful place…I wonder if I might have a kiss. Would you mind?"

"Not at all." She turned her face up toward him, feeling a bit uncertain but trying to not let it show. She wasn't sure what to do.

Leon gathered her in his arms, ever so gently. He bent his head and brushed his lips over her forehead, her cheeks and mouth. Her eyes fluttered closed and her arms came around his body. "Esther, you are so sweet, so beautiful." He kissed her mouth.

It felt right. She had never been kissed like this before. His lips felt warm and tasted sweet, his arms were strong, yet gentle. She knew he would never hurt her. Something inside her began to stir. He pulled his lips away and smiled at her as he continued to hold her.

"Thank you," he said. "I've wanted to kiss your sweet lips." He helped her up into the buggy then jogged to the other side and joined her. He turned her chin up, gave her another smile and a quick peck on the lips. He held her quietly for a moment. *Oh Esther, you have no idea how precious you are to God and to me.*

Grasping the reins with one hand, he smiled, "Shall we?" Leon gave the horse a little click-click sound with his mouth. Once more, they were underway, holding hands and snuggling under the quilts.

Esther was a bit breathless to be with this man of the world, so handsome and strong, yet gentle. Somehow the twelve years difference in their ages didn't seem to matter now, as much as she had feared.

Leon pulled into her driveway and up to her back door. "Let me help you down." He offered his hand. He kept her hand in his as they walked up to her door. "Thank you," he said, "When can I see you again?"

"Thank you for very nice time," she said. "Mother would like you to come for Sunday dinner after church tomorrow. Doris is having dinner with Bill and his family."

"Very well, I will see you after church. Would you like to ride home with me in my buggy?"

"Oh, yes, I would."

"It's agreed then. Tomorrow after church. Goodbye Esther."

"Goodbye, Leon."

He gave her another quick kiss, turned and hastened to his buggy. He wanted to yell and throw his hat in the air. He whistled and relived their kisses all the way home.

***

CHAPTER FOURTEEN – Sunday Dinner

Tooling along in the buggy with Leon spoke volumes to everyone who saw the two of them leave the church even though they remained separated, eyes straight ahead in a circumspect manner. When they passed the last house on the edge of town, they turned to each other and laughed. "Scoot over," grinned Leon as he patted the seat beside him. Esther obliged. "This is better," he said as he put his arm around her.

Leon began singing one of the rousing church school songs they had sung earlier. Esther joined in and started another. When finished Leon thought of another, and so it continued until they reached the house.

"I do believe we beat your family home, Esther."

"I think you're right, but they should be home before too long. Father likes to hang around after church and talk shop with his buddies. Hunger pangs should bring them along soon."

"Then, let's not waste any time," he said and put his arm around her. She lifted her face and he brushed a few stray hairs back into place. He kissed her on the nose and smiled down at her. She smiled and rested her head on his broad chest. She could hear his heart thumping. Leon encircled her with both arms, stroked her back and planted kisses on top her head. "Give me one kiss, sweetheart and then we will go inside. All right?"

She lifted her face for a kiss and let her eyes drift closed. He sought her mouth and pressed his lips on hers. She kissed him back. He tickled her lips just a little bit with his tongue, gave her a squeeze and released her. "Mm," she said. Leon bounded down and around to help her alight. They entered the house through the kitchen door. She took his dress coat and hat and hung them in the backroom.

"I need to go out and tie up my horse. I'll be right back."

"If you want to unhitch him, you can leave him in the horse barn."

"All right, good idea as I'll probably be here for two or three hours."

"If you see Dad's farm-hand around you can ask him to do it."

"Very well, I'll be back in ten minutes." Leon grabbed a work coat off a hook and was out the door.

Esther checked the roast in the oven, added the potatoes and carrots which were waiting, washed and ready, and began to assemble the dinnerware for setting the table. Mother had a couple of side dishes planned but they would only take minutes, better to leave them until she heard their rig approaching. Esther shook up some flour and water for the gravy, filled the water glasses and set the condiments on the table. Seeing nothing further to do, she stood watching out the window as Leon approached the house. She opened the door for him. "Come in, Leon, find everything you needed?"

Leon shucked the coat and hung it on the rack. "Everything's fine. I watered Gibraltar and took the liberty of giving him a little of your father's feed. He quieted right down in the stall and started munching. I won't have to worry about him until I'm ready to leave."

"Let's pour ourselves some coffee and go sit in the parlor until my parents arrive," suggested Esther.

"I would just as soon sit here in the kitchen," Leon stated when he remembered the uncomfortable parlor settee and opted instead to pull out a chair at the breakfast table.

"Your wish is my command, your majesty." Esther dropped a curtsey and they both laughed remembering yesterday's picnic. She placed two brimming cups on the table.

Leon added sugar and began to stir. "Wasn't yesterday fun? Maybe we can visit the park again in the spring."

Esther's face fell. "Um, I won't be around next spring, Leon."

"What do you mean you won't be around? Of course you'll be around."

"No. I will be going east to stay with my aunt. I'm leaving after school dismisses for the holidays."

"But… Esther," he stammered. "We are just getting to know each other. I am becoming fond of you and I thought you felt the same way."

Esther looked down at her hands as she fiddled with her coffee cup. "Well, there is a reason I must leave. This is for the best, believe me. Maybe after I return we can resume seeing each other…if you are still free then." Esther raised her eyes, remembering Winifred, looking completely stricken.

"Esther, your father told me about the…er…reason you think you have to leave. It doesn't matter to me. I want to be here for you. I want to take care of you. Do you understand?"

Esther gasped and covered her mouth. "Oh my g--goodness, he told you! You've known all along."

"Not all along, but, yes, he told me. Believe me, Esther, it really does not matter to me."

In shock and humiliation, Esther hurried from the room, flew up the stairs and threw herself on the bed. Great sobs wracked her body. *How can it not matter? I've been such a fool! I should never have gone out with him. How dare he pity me? I can't believe my parents would betray my secret. I feel horrible!* In despair, she buried her face in the pillow and wept.

    ***

Millie came in the kitchen door. She moved to hang up her coat and tie on an apron. Leon sat morosely staring out the window. "Afternoon, Leon. We'll have dinner ready just as soon as Walter comes in. Looks like Esther has everything under control. Don't move while I get this hot roaster out of the oven. I wouldn't want to burn you." She didn't seem to notice Leon wasn't paying her any mind.

She poked the potatoes with a fork. "Mm, not quite done. We'll give them a few more minutes." She slid the roaster back in the oven, set the vegetables on the stove to commence warming, got out her chilled cream and begin whipping it for a Jello topping. Just then Walter came in from unhitching the horses. "Go ahead and get washed up, Walter. I'll have dinner ready in about ten minutes." She grabbed a cup of coffee and sat down with Leon. "You're quiet today, Leon."

"Oh, sorry." Leon straightened and turned to look at her.

"How was your class today?"

"Fine."

Millie worked hard at small talk until Walter joined them.

"There are some tantalizing odors coming out of this kitchen, Millie. I'm starved. When do we eat?" asked Walter.

"Almost ready," said Millie. "Waiting for the vegetables to soften and then I'll make the gravy. There are some pickles on the table. Can I get you one?"

"I'll wait for the meat and potatoes, thank you. So, Leon, how is the courting going? Where is Esther, anyway? Still upstairs? She's taking her sweet time about it."

"I'm afraid I may have ruined everything," answered Leon. "She's probably upstairs sobbing her eyes out."

"Oh my," said Millie. "Not good at all. I'll go to her."

"Perhaps it would be better to leave her alone for a while," suggested Leon. "I'm afraid I let the cat out of the bag."

"You don't mean about her pregnancy."

"Yes," Leon nodded. "She surprised me by telling me she was moving east with her aunt and I just, sort of...I don't remember how I said it. Next thing I knew she was crying and running upstairs. I'm sure she thinks I have misled her. I think she may blame you a little bit, too, Walter."

Walter and Millie exchanged knowing looks. Walter made the first attempt, "Now, Leon, don't blame yourself. Neither one of us did a single thing wrong."

"Walter's right, Leon," Millie added. "You can't blame yourself. Everyone is just trying to help in a difficult situation. Understand, women in her condition are a bundle of nerves. You have to make allowances. I'm sure she feels shamed and devastated when you, of all people, know about it. She probably thinks we have blabbed to the whole town."

"Let's get dinner started," said Walter. "She'll be down when she's ready."

***

Three pairs of eyes looked up from their plates as Esther came down the stairs. Her eyes were red from crying and her hair was hanging half undone. "Come here, kitten." Walter held out an arm. Esther moved into his embrace. "Now, I want you to forget about your humiliation for a minute. Okay? We all know this is tough for you. We're just doing our best to help you. Okay?"

Esther nodded and sniffed.

Walter continued, "You need to know, no one outside of our family and Leon knows, believe me. It was only right I told Leon. After all, he came to me and asked for permission to court you, as he should. We have to respect him. It was only fair he understands the situation, we owed him the truth. He gave his word of honor to keep it a secret, no matter how your courtship turned out and I believe him. Leon is a man of integrity and his intentions are honorable. He told me your pregnancy didn't matter to him and I trust him completely. Has he been treating you right, kitten?" Esther nodded. "See? There you are. Everything's going to be all right. We have to trust God, don't we?" affirmed Walter.

She wiped her eyes.

"Now, honey, why don't you sit down over there next to Leon and we'll all have dessert. What do you say?"

Esther nodded and moved around the table. Leon rose to pull out her chair. He gave her shoulder a squeeze.

***

CHAPTER FIFTEEN – The Dance

The traditional Christmas dance was well underway when Leon drew up and tossed the reins to the waiting boy. He helped Esther down and they ascended the stairs.

Fiddle music and banjos assailed their ears. They lingered on the sidelines for a minute taking it all in and adjusting to the dimness of the lighting. Lines of dancers moved forward and back, twirled, then moved forward and passed through, then turned and faced again. Couples were laughing when they missed a step or bumped into each other, not always by accident.

The room was gaily decorated with garlands of pine boughs, silver bells, huge red bows and mirrors. Esther's best party dress was a demure pale blue with dainty silver stripes, white tatted lace around the hem and neckline and puff sleeves. Leon looked devastatingly handsome in a dark suit which fit like a glove across his broad shoulders and muscled thighs.

Esther felt uncertain, for Leon seemed to know a good half of the people, while Esther only spotted a few she recognized. Several people waved at Leon as they danced past. Esther's eyes glazed over when she saw Winifred dancing with an unfamiliar tall man.

Winifred looked enchanting in a fashionable, bright red slinky dress, cut low in the neckline. Winifred and her escort cut out of the line of dance and headed toward Leon and Esther. She placed two hands on Leon's shoulders, gave him a kiss on the check, leaned into him and purred, "Darling, I haven't seen you in ages. Who's been keeping you busy lately, hmm?" She batted her long, thick lashes at Leon and slanted a look at Esther.

Leon leaned over her, "Now, Winnie, pull in your claws."

"I can't imagine what you mean, Lee, darling. Can you join us later at the house? We are having a little gathering after the dance," said Winifred, implying there would be no other people at all. "You'll be there, won't you darling?"

"Not this time, Winifred, as you can see I'm otherwise occupied."
He motioned toward Esther. "You've met Esther Dodes, I presume."

Winifred pursed her lips in a pretty little pout, "All right, dear boy,
if you promise to save me a waltz for later. Deal?"

"No deal, Winifred. Now you run along and join your many
admirers." Leon let go of her waist and offered a hand to Esther.
"Shall we dance?" Without a word Esther laid her hand in his and
they glided off. "Pay no attention to Winifred," Leon offered. "She
has her act down pat."

"I wanted to scratch her eyes out," admitted Esther.

Leon expertly twirled her around a corner. "So, you're a little bit
jealous. Ah, a good sign." He pulled her a little closer, laid his cheek
on the top of her head and inhaled her perfume. "Mm, your hair
smells good."

"It's Doris's shampoo and rinse. You like?"

"Mm, I like. You feel delightful, too."

"You're a smooth dancer." Esther tried to keep her feet in step.

"You are so tiny. I could dance with you all night and never tire.
Tell me you won't dance with anyone else, just with me."

"I wouldn't want to be rude?"

"You might, but who cares?"

"You have a point."

"Don't forget who's taking you home."

"Whoever do you mean, sir?"

"You are my wench, and don't you forget it!" he admonished and
launched into a series of dizzying twirls.

***

Next day Walter caught up with Leon before they entered the
church. "Leon, may I have a word with you?"

"Certainly," Leon agreed.

"Let's step over here for a minute. I'd like to speak with you privately. Leon, I'm afraid we're running out of time. Esther's Aunt Lily has written and wants her to come right away, as early as next week."

"What do you suggest I do?"

"Well, it's up to you, son. If you want her, you need to move fast, or else wait until she returns from Connecticut… if she returns."

"My heart tells me I can't let her go, but you know I am not in a position to support a wife and baby, yet, Walter."

"Well then, I think you need to tell her how you feel. Be honest with her. If she'll have you, a quick and quiet wedding would be best. After you are wed you can stay with her mother and me during her confinement. We can provide you with a room. And you can go on working at Hubbard's until you are ready to buy a spread of your own."

"Very generous of you, Walter," Leon answered, "but you know I'd rather provide for my own wife and child."

"You will, son, you will. Granted, I know this would not be an ideal arrangement. Are you still willing to claim the child as your own?" Leon nodded. "You do have a choice, you know," Walter continued. "If you prefer she can go out east, put the baby up for adoption, and when she comes home, you would still have a chance to start with a clean slate, in your own home, begetting your own children."

"I suppose that recourse might be good for my reputation, but I can't believe it would be best for Esther. My mind is made up. I'll ask her to marry me, even though I'm not sure she's ready."

"Son, if you want her, she'll be ready." Walter clapped him on the back.

Leon nodded, "I'll drive over this afternoon." They turned together and entered the church.

***

CHAPTER SIXTEEN – The Proposal

Walter dropped his napkin on his plate. "Delicious dinner, Millie." He patted his stomach. "I'm afraid I ate more than I should. I'll have to go outside and work this off chopping some wood."

"Nonsense," Doris protested. "You don't have an ounce of fat on your body. Can I get you some coffee and dessert, Father?"

"No, thank you, Doris. Well, on second thought, I guess I would like some coffee, but no dessert right now, thank you. Then you can run along and get ready for Bill's visit. Mother and I want to speak with Esther for a minute."

   ***

Walter idly stirred his coffee and cleared his throat. He looked up at Esther.

"Honey, your mother and I are aware you have a new beau. We want you to know we approve of Leon's paying attention to you."

"Yes, Father. I understand."

"Are you fond of Leon?"

"Yes, Father."

Millie asked, as gently as possible, "Are you in love with him, Esther?"

"I'm fond of him. We have enjoyed each other's company. He is a perfect gentleman. But, love? How do I know?"

"Well, if you don't know, then you aren't in love. But it is possible, isn't it, someday?"

"I don't know, Mother. I have no one to compare with Leon. I've had lots of high school friends, but Leon is the only serious beau I've ever had, and we've been out together, what...three times?"

Millie was silent.

"Here's the reality, Esther," explained Walter. "Leon is old enough to know his mind. He has had plenty of experience with women and knows what he wants in a wife. I believe it is possible Leon plans to propose marriage to you."

Esther gasped, "Surely not, not so soon."

"Yes, it will be soon. Not because he is in a rush to wed, but because you announced you are leaving in less than two weeks' time. Leon realizes he must act now before you leave. Do you understand?"

"Um, well, I guess so."

"We think you should give serious consideration to accepting his offer."

"But, why can't he wait until I come back?"

"Are you coming back? So far, you haven't said."

"Well, I might...and I might not. I don't know what I'll do."

Millie spoke, "The facts are, in this day and age, it isn't easy for a woman on her own in the world. Maybe by next year we women will have the vote, but I'm not sure whether anything will change."

"Especially a woman with no particular skills, who also has a baby," added Walter.

Esther looked crestfallen. "What are you saying?"

"Darling, we aren't telling you what to do. It is your decision, but we wanted you to have a little warning time to think this through and decide what you will say if Leon pops the question sometime in the next two weeks. If you love him, or if you think you could love him, this could be the answer to your prayers.

"Now, we want you to take all the time you need right now to think this through before Leon comes to call. Your mother and I will be right here. Feel free to come and talk to us...whatever you need. We'll enjoy clearing the table together, won't we Millie? How about you wash and I'll dry?" He rose from the table as Esther went upstairs.

"Hold on, Walter, I want to get a picture of this."

76

He laughed and gave her a playful pat on the butt. She pretended to dodge him and threw him the towel.

***

Esther was asleep on her bed when Leon arrived, riding Gibraltar.

Millie welcomed him at the door. "Come on in, Leon. I'm afraid Esther is sound asleep. Poor dear, I guess she needed it."

"Ah, well, Madam, I trust I didn't keep her out too late last evening."

"Not at all. No, I think this is just a natural sleepiness for any woman in her condition."

"Yes, of course. Perhaps I will ride back to my place, finish up the chores and come back this evening."

"I'm sorry to disappoint you."

"Not at all, madam. This is probably better, anyway."

"We usually have a light supper on Sunday evenings, about seven. Plan on joining us."

"Thank you, I'll ride over."

"Very well, goodbye, Leon."

"Good afternoon, ma'am. I'll see you later."

***

The family was in the dining room playing board games when Leon returned. Esther greeted him at the door with a hug and a kiss.

"Well done my dear, I like a nice warm welcome," Leon grinned.

"We wenches catch on quickly, your Majesty." They stood smiling in each other's arms. "Are you terribly hungry? We can eat right away if you are."

"I'm in no hurry. Let's sit and visit for a while first. Is there anywhere private we can talk?"

"Well, we can sit right here in the kitchen or we can move into the parlor. In either case we would need to close the door."

"Maybe if we stay right here, it will be less obvious." He reached behind her and quietly closed the dining room door.

"Come sit with me, Esther. I have something very important to ask you." He pulled out two chairs, arranged the chairs so they faced each other, helped Esther into one chair and took the other for himself. Leon took her hands in his. "Esther, in this short time we have been going out together, I have grown very fond of you. Do I dare hope you return the sentiments?"

"Yes, I am fond of you, too, Leon."

"I know it is much too soon to be asking you this dear, but do you think in time you might be able to grow to love me? Please don't answer right away. Give it some thought and answer honestly."

"Yes, I think it is possible, but I do not know for certain any more than *you* do."

"Many good solid marriages have been built on less. I'm willing to try and I hope you are too. You know me better than you realize. I've been honest and open with you. Your parents have known me for more than ten years and I'm sure they approve of our marriage. I have money saved, almost enough to buy our own small home, and your father has promised to help us get started.

"Also, you can stay right here until the baby is born and I will stay with you every night. Once you are back on your feet and the baby is doing well, we can move into our own little house. I want to be the father to your baby, Esther."

Leon rose, pushed back his chair, lowered on one knee, clung to her hand, looked her straight in the eye and asked, "Esther Elizabeth, will you do me the honor of becoming my wife?"

"Oh...oh my!" Esther pressed her fingers to her lips and gazed at Leon in amazement.

"Darling, please say yes," he implored.

"I don't know what to say." She bit her lip and thought of what her father had advised her. "Yes, I *do* know what to say. I will say yes, Leon, I will marry you and thank you very much for asking."

"Oh my sweet little bird. You have made me the happiest man alive. May I kiss you?"

Esther smiled shyly and nodded. Leon rose, gently coaxed her to her feet, gathered her in his arms and kissed her with all his heart.

"I have something in my pocket for you, darling." He reached in his pocket, pulled out a small velvet covered box and opened it for her to see a beautiful diamond solitaire set in a gold band. Her eyes grew in wonder. Leon lifted the ring out of the box with great care, took her left hand in his and slipped the ring on her finger.

She held her hand out to admire the ring, wiggled her finger and watched the ring sparkle in the light. "Oh it is beautiful, Leon, and thank you so much. I love it!" She reached up to kiss him again.

"Let's go tell your folks, shall we?" He took her hand and, wreathed in smiles, they walked together into the dining room.

Esther beamed at her mother. "Mama see what Leon has done. He has asked me to marry him." She held out her left hand. The rock on her finger dazzled almost as much as her smile.

Millie rose and came to her, arms outstretched. Amid hugs and kisses she exclaimed, "Oh, Esther, what a beautiful ring! I'm so happy for you!" She turned toward Leon. "For both of you!" she opened her arms for Leon, too, and smiled at them through her tears.

Walter shook Leon's hand and hugged his daughter. "I wish the two of you all the happiness in the world. Congratulations, both of you. This calls for a celebration. Do we have anything in the house, Millie? I wish to propose a toast."

"Well, there may be one bottle of wine hidden away down in the fruit cellar. I'll go look for it."

"I'll help you open it," offered Leon.

While they were gone, Bill and Doris drove up. "Ask Bill to come in a minute, Doris. We have an announcement."

"Sure, Dad. I'll tell him." She was off to catch Bill.

Esther and Walter were alone. "Well now young lady, you've made the right decision. I'm sure of it."

"Oh, Daddy, I hope so. I thought it over, just as you asked. Thank you for telling me in advance. It gave me time to think it through. I have to do this, Daddy, for all of our sakes. Now my baby will have a real father, instead of o…" She caught herself before she almost blurted out the name, "the horrible man who raped me."

"You made the right decision," Walter repeated. "I would never have allowed it if I wasn't sure you will fall in love eventually."

"I hope you're right."

"Esther, some day you are going to have to name the man who did this to you. None of us will ever rest peacefully again until he is put away."

***

PART TWO

CHAPTER SEVENTEEN – The Wedding Trip

Doris exclaimed over the last garment carefully folded and placed in the suitcase. "This is so pretty! What lovely imported lace! I envy you all these nice things. Aren't you the lucky one, Esther?"

"Yes, I suppose I am," said Esther, a bit uncertain.

"Oh, but you are," insisted Doris. "Everything is working out beyond your wildest dreams. What more could a girl want?"

"Well, there are a few things."

"Like what?"

"It would have been nice to finish school before I became saddled with a husband and baby."

"Well, how important is a diploma? It's just a piece of paper which eventually gets lost in a drawer. Who cares? No one cares. No one will even know but you. You will have what is really important to a woman, a handsome husband and cute little babies to play with."

"I suppose so." Esther's reply held little conviction.

"And now you are going off for an elopement and brief honeymoon."

"Oh well, just one night, but maybe you're right."

"Don't tell me you're frightened of Leon."

"Maybe, a little."

"I see. Has mother told you what your wedding night will be like?"

"The only thing I know is what I experienced when the man attacked me."

"Oh dear, this is not good. Esther, you are going to have to relax and forget what happened."

"Easy for you to say, but I don't think I can do it."

"I see what you're saying. Well, let me assure you. What you experience with Leon will be nothing like what happened to you before, nothing at all. Believe me, you will love it."

"How do you know so much?"

Doris blushed. "Well, Bill and I have experimented some. I know it is going to be wonderful. You see how Mother and Father carry on when they think we aren't looking."

"I wish I could have a marriage like theirs."

"You will, darling, you will. Trust me." Doris gave Esther a reassuring hug.

Esther spent a sleepless night, pondering those things and worrying about her ability to be a good wife.

***

Leon came for her the next morning. He was driving his matched grays hitched to a handsome carriage. He wanted his bride to be comfortable and warm. They would drive half the way to Ionia today and stop at an Inn for the night. They could have taken the interurban train from Jackson to Lansing, then a hired carriage to Ionia, but Leon preferred his own conveyance.

Millie, Walter and Doris were on hand to see the couple off. Leon quipped, "Here, I thought I was going to have to bring my bride down from her room by way of a ladder."

Walter caught the mood and retorted, "I'll have you know my shotgun is ready in case you decide to back out."

"Not a chance, friend, not a chance!" Leon chuckled.

"Take good care of her, Leon. She's mighty precious to me," Walter intoned.

Millie wiped a tear away with her apron. "Here, give us all a hug before you go." Hugs and kisses followed all around.

"Up you go, dearest," said Leon as he boosted Esther into the carriage. "I'll be up on top. Just knock twice if you need to stop. Okay?"

Esther nodded. She took a seat by the window and gazed out at her family, her thoughts in disarray. With a click-click to the horses and a little flip on the reins, they were off. Esther waved and watched out the window until her home and family faded from view. With a sigh she leaned back against the seat cushion and picked up her needlework. It would be a long journey.

Leon had plenty of time to reflect on his situation. Esther was so different from Winifred. For all practical purposes he would have an innocent bride, physically unprepared for everything marriage implied. She was pregnant without quite understanding how it all happened.

Walter had filled him in on the details of her rape. *Esther is trying to be brave, but it's just a front,* Leon thought. I know she's scared silly. Leon couldn't help worrying about the coming wedding night. I'll have to overcome her reluctance, somehow. He would have to be ever so gentle and make absolutely sure his wife enjoyed it. All his powers of control would be called into play. *Dear God, I'm not sure if I can handle this. Without your help I'll be lacking for sure.*

Well, God, you got me into this mess. Don't desert me, now, was a prayer he breathed more times than he could count, even though he believed God valued faith more than repetitious prayers.

Esther felt almost dizzy from the hurricane of activity and changes in her life in the last few weeks, all because of one devastating rape over in minutes. The unintended consequences would last a lifetime. Already, lives were irrevocably changed. A tiny life grew in her womb. *Are you a boy or a girl? What will you be like? Will I ever tell you who your real father is? Oh how I despise the repulsive man and what he did to me! Lord, please guide me. I cannot do this without your help.*

Ever since it happened Otis had stayed out of sight in the barns, but sometimes Esther sensed someone watching her. It gave her the creeps. No! She must never tell. *Oh, God, what if the baby is like its father?* Esther tried to quiet her thoughts and concentrate on her stitches. It was no use. Just when her needle touched the right spot, a bump of the carriage caused the stitch to go astray. She pulled out as many stitches as she put in. Esther sighed, laid the needlework on the seat beside her, closed her eyes and tried to catch up on lost sleep.

***

They reached Ionia the next day after an uneventful night spent in separate rooms at an unremarkable inn. Pastor Lohengrin and his wife could not have been more gracious. They really enjoyed pampering young couples in love.

Mrs. Lohengrin showed Esther to her room. "Oh, how lovely!" Esther exclaimed and clapped her hands. The four-poster bed was dressed in a dainty white coverlet with tiny blue and lavender flowers and topped with a mound of pillows in the same fabric, some edged with rows of tatted lace. A bay window with cushions beckoned her to curl up with a book. The window overlooked a manicured garden which would be glorious in summertime. A stack of fluffy towels sat on a washstand next to a white china pitcher and bowl. Little carved soaps and bottles of mysterious perfumes and lotions lined up in front of a Cheval glass mirror. Esther turned toward her hostess, "Thank you. This is so much more than I expected."

"You are quite welcome, my dear. Your mother and I are old friends going way back farther than I care to remember. Besides we like to make our little brides comfortable. You will need a good night's rest before your wedding day," she chirped as she turned to leave. "If there is anything you need, anything at all, just ring the little bell. Supper won't be until six o'clock so feel free to get some rest. I will call you in plenty of time to get ready.

***

Next morning Esther awoke to the sound of voices. Following small town tradition, the Lohengrins had enlisted a few women from their congregation to assist with wedding preparations, serve as witnesses and help clean up afterward. Esther took care of her morning ablutions, while Pastor and Leon got ready in a different part of the house. Mrs. Lohengrin bustled around directing activities, popping in at the last minute to assist the bride. She fussed over Esther's veil, adjusting it on her head and arranging the folds of fine netting edged with expensive imported lace. "You look absolutely beautiful, my dear. Look at this lace! So pretty! Yours is the most beautiful wedding dress I've seen in a long time."

The bodice of Esther's white silk dress was completely covered with matching embroidered lace in a bolero style. The sleeves were lace lined with satin. A row of tiny eyelet embroidery edged the hem of the ankle length skirt. Her feet and legs were clad in stockings of white lace and petite satin slippers. Esther's thick mane of chestnut hair fell down her right shoulder in one fat twisted curl, reaching almost to her waist. "Thank you, Mrs. Lohengrin," breathed Esther. "This dress was made in Paris and sent over by my great-grandmother. It has been carefully preserved in my hope chest for many years. I believe the lace goes back several generations."

"Here Esther is the finishing touch. These flowers are for you. Pastor Lohengrin likes to provide all of his brides their bouquet."

"Oh, it's beautiful," breathed Esther as she buried her nose in its fragrance. "Thank you so much."

"You are ever so welcome, dear. Now I believe you are ready. I will go ahead and alert the others and you can come down in a couple minutes." She kissed Esther on the cheek. "Good luck, dear."

Esther stood at the top of the open staircase until she was certain everyone was in place and quietly waiting. She squared her shoulders, took a deep breath and slowly descended the stairs.

Leon awaited her at the foot of the staircase, his eyes on her. He offered his arm, bent his head and whispered, "You look ravishing.

Come with me, my dear." With his other hand he reached up and twisted a mock mustache out of view of the assembled witnesses. This evoked the hoped-for result as Esther relaxed and almost laughed aloud. They turned and proceeded toward a flower bedecked bower where they stood facing the clergyman. Leon beamed down at her and gave her hand a little pat. "Courage," he whispered softly for her ears only.

"Dearly beloved, we are gathered here together…" Pastor Lohengrin intoned the traditional words entirely from memory. His voice began to fade out as Esther's knees turned to rubber. Leon could feel her hands quivering. She leaned toward him and he put his arm around her to give her strength. It was a relief to place her knees on the kneeling stool for the blessing. From here she would not have far to fall.

"… Those whom God has joined together, let no man put asunder. I now pronounce you husband and wife." The pastor's voice faded back in. "You may now kiss the bride." *It's over and I don't remember a thing,* thought Esther. Leon helped her up, took her in his arms and thoroughly kissed her. The kitchen helpers who had slipped in to observe burst into applause. Esther found her voice, "Are we married, now?"

"We most certainly are, Mrs. Douglas," said Leon, as he smiled at her and held her tight. "You said all the right words, in all the right places, in front of these witnesses. Congratulations, darling." He let go with his right hand while holding her with his left. Leon began shaking hands with Pastor Lohengrin and the others, while they crowded around to kiss the bride. The elderly ladies even went so far as to kiss the groom.

The pastor gave Esther a hearty kiss on the cheek. "I never pass up a chance to kiss a beautiful lady." He pumped Leon's hand. "Congratulations. You are a very lucky fellow."

A maid in a starched black uniform with a white cap and wearing a frilly white apron entered the room and rang a silver bell for attention.

"Excuse me, ladies and gentlemen. Breakfast is served, if you would please come this way." Esther and Leon were shown to a long table covered with white linen and lace, set with fine china, crystal and silver, and gleaming with candlelight.

Everyone gathered around the table and Pastor Lohengrin said the blessing. The maid filled the wine glasses and the toasts began, with much frivolity. The wine was just enough to relax Esther and she began to enjoy herself. Several delicious courses were served, the final one being a lovely miniature wedding cake in several layers, decorated with white frosting and pink roses, with a tiny bride and groom on top.

From time to time the guests demanded a kiss whereupon Leon and Esther stood up and demonstrated how it's done. At length the dishes were cleared away to make way for dessert. Esther was shown where to stand to toss her bouquet. Pastor Lohengrin's elderly widowed mother caught the bouquet, amid much hilarity, as she was in her nineties. "It's never too late," she boasted. Esther and Leon cut the first piece of cake and fed each other a bite. They returned to their places while the maid served cake to everyone.

In due course, it was time for them to take their leave. Esther thanked her hosts sincerely and profusely. Leon couldn't resist a lame joke, "Thank you so much. This was the loveliest wedding I've ever had. Of course it was the only wedding I've ever had, but still it had to be the loveliest." Esther smiled and thought, *oh no, this is a side of Leon I haven't seen. Lord, spare me.*

Soon they were out the door in a shower of rice and well wishes. Leon's carriage awaited them in front of the house, bedecked with paper roses, streamers and a "Just Married" sign. Even the matched grays had braids and white ribbons in their hair. A hired coachman was perched in place, so Leon could join his bride inside the coach. He handed her in, took his place next to her and reached around her to pull down the shades. "Come here, Mrs. Douglas," he said and she moved into his arms without hesitation. He reached up to unpin her veil and set it aside. Gently he smoothed her brow and smiled, "You were so beautiful, today, Esther, my love. May I kiss the bride?"

"Please do, quickly," she answered.

He lowered his head and fixed his lips to hers. She responded by wrapping her arms around his neck. He deepened the kiss and pressed her body to his strong frame. At length he carefully drew away and knocked on the ceiling to signal the coachman to proceed. "Here we go, darling."

Esther turned in his arms and leaned back against his chest. Leon snuggled her up close and they talked quietly about the wedding. From time to time he turned her around for another sizzling kiss and then settled her back against him. They compared notes on their separate experiences. Both agreed it was an amazing and unexpected pleasure. "The Lohengrins were so kind. They went all out to make things right for us. We shall be forever grateful."

"Your gown is amazing, Esther. Did you whip it up in the last two days?"

Esther laughed, "This gown is very old."

"Oh, really? I would never have guessed. It is beautiful. You were beautiful, and you *are* beautiful."

"My dress was made in Paris for my great-grandmother. It has been kept for me in my hope chest, for years," she explained.

"How interesting! So, tell me why wasn't the gown in Doris' hope chest? She is the elder daughter, after all."

Esther giggled, "I was the lucky one because I am smaller than Doris. She couldn't get into the dress. It fit me perfectly."

"You are perfect, all right, just my size."

Leon had reserved the bridal suite at a quiet inn just outside of Lansing. He helped Esther down and tossed a coin to the boy waiting to take their bags. The innkeeper and his wife were waiting to greet them. He bowed slightly and held the door. "Good evening, Mr. and Mrs. Douglas. Welcome to our establishment. Your rooms are all ready for you. I trust you will find everything in order. I will show you right up. Follow me, this way, please."

The innkeeper opened their room and gestured them in with a small flourish. "This is our very best room, sir and madam. If there is anything you need please ring for the maid. Your supper is set out for you in the parlor. A warm bath is ready in the dressing room and a fire is going in the fireplace. I believe you are all set. I will leave you now. Enjoy." He bowed himself out and closed the door with a click.

This time there was only one room with a huge bed and adjoining parlor. They were alone. Suddenly Esther felt small and adrift. Leon paced the length of both rooms and back. He turned toward Esther. "Here, let me help you out of your beautiful dress, Little One." She turned and he began to work on the tiny buttons down the length of her back. Esther pulled the sleeves off and the dress pooled around her feet. She stood there in her chemise, pantaloons garters and stockings while Leon carefully hung her dress up in the wardrobe. "We can't let anything happen to this special dress, can we? After all, our daughter may want to wear it one day."

"I suppose," said Esther. "I never thought about it."

"Well, I guess there is no hurry to think about it, is there? We don't have any daughters, as yet."

"No, we don't."

Leon hung his jacket next to the dress and removed his shoes. "Come, darling, let us to bed. I want to love you." Esther froze in place. "Are you worried, my dear? Please don't be. Here, let me hold you." Leon surrounded her with his arms. She stood stiff and unyielding. "You're trembling. Don't be afraid of me, Little One. I would never, ever hurt you."

"I'm sorry. I don't mean to be afraid. I just can't help myself."

"It's all right. Nothing bad is going to happen. I will take care of you, always. I promise you. You are under my protection. Nothing will ever harm you or hurt you again. Trust me."

Esther sighed and leaned her head on his chest.

"There now darling, just relax against me. Here is what I suggest we do: You see the big chair over there by the fireplace? Why don't we get the wine off the table in the parlor and one of the blankets and cuddle up in the chair. It will remind us of our picnic, don't you think?"

She nodded and he had everything gathered in a flash, including removing his socks and trousers and unbuttoning his shirt. "Now let me pour some wine in these two glasses, and then you come and sit on my lap." Soon they were snuggled in the big chair, sipping wine and staring into the fire. Leon nuzzled her neck and planted little kisses from time to time. He stroked her arms.

"Darling, I want you to feel free to touch me in any way you like, touch me anywhere, do you understand me? Anywhere! I'm your husband now. In time, we are going to know each other's bodies even better than our own."

She reached around and laid her hand on his cheek. Next she rubbed the outside of his leg.

"There you go, honey. Keep doing whatever feels good to you." He gave her a peck on the cheek and patted her arm. "Does this feel good, darling?"

"Yes."

He lifted her hair and planted a row of kisses on the back of her neck and down her spine as far as he could reach. "How about this?"

"It's okay."

"I like what you are wearing now. Not sure what you call this garment. Very pretty." He caressed her body. "Do you have more surprises like this for me in your suitcase? Hmm?" He raised the wine glass to her mouth. "Have a sip?"

"Thank you." She took the glass and helped herself.

"Are you happy, Esther?"

"Um, happy? Well, I suppose so."

"I'm so happy, darling, I could fly. Thank you for making me a happy man." He squeezed her and stroked her hair. "Your hair is so beautiful, Esther. Kiss me, darling."

Esther half turned and kissed him.

"Open your mouth a little bit, Esther."

Esther opened her mouth a crack. Leon kissed her again and tickled her lips with his tongue. He held the kiss and deepened it as much as she allowed. He placed his hand on her breast and felt her nipple with his thumb. Esther held herself perfectly still. Leon moved his hand to her female area and Esther stiffened. He moved his hand around to her backside and rubbed it gently and continued to kiss her. Things weren't going as quickly as he had hoped.

"Would you like some more wine, or would you prefer to check out the supper?"

Esther leaped out of his lap. "Let's have supper."

After supper, Esther decided she would take a bath. Leon prided himself on being a patient man; but this notion was being put to an extreme test tonight. After her bath Esther emerged wrapped in a flannel nightgown with high neck and long sleeves.

Leon looked at her apparition and bit his tongue. *No,* he thought, *this has to stop, but how can I approach the subject.* "Esther, honey, don't you think your night gown is a little too warm for tonight?"

"No, once the fire goes out, it will get cold in here. I always wear a warm nightgown to bed."

"But, darling, this is our wedding night. I planned to keep you warm with my body next to yours."

"Oh, would you rather I changed into something else?"

"Well, what I was thinking was no nightgown at all."

"Oh."

"I assume you understand what married couples do on their wedding night?"

"How am I supposed to know?" she snapped. "It's not as if I've ever been married, you know."

"Of course not, how silly of me! Will you allow me to teach you?"

"All right, I guess so."

"Atta girl. Good. Now, the first thing you do is remove your gown and get into bed next to me. I will turn out the lamps and blow out the candles and do the same. Then we are going to hold each other and kiss and feel each other's bodies. There's more but let's do this much first."

Esther dived under the covers, wiggled around for a couple minutes, threw her nightgown over the side and lay still, watching him undress. Completely naked, now, Leon took care of the lights. Then he lay down beside her and took her into his arms.

"Now, we go on to step two. We hold each other. We move our hands over each other's bodies and we kiss." Leon kissed her, held her close and stroked her in as many places as he could. Esther was quite adept at keeping her intimate places just out of reach. The few times he managed to touch her there, she quickly wiggled out of his touch. Her respiration rate remained slow and steady. She made not a sound. Once again he tried to touch her intimately.

"Tell me, Little One, do you like me to touch you there?"

"I'd rather you didn't."

"Darling, it is important you get used to it. Otherwise I will not be able to prepare you for the marital act. If you aren't properly prepared, it will hurt you."

"I know how it hurts."

"But, it won't hurt when it is your husband. If you will allow me to do it properly, you will like it."

"Can't we just do it quickly and get it over with?"

"No not really. It needs to be slow and gentle to be good."

"I'd rather you would just go ahead and do it. Then I can go to sleep. We can both go to sleep. When you are asleep you won't care if I wear my nightgown, will you?"

"Not so much, no," he admitted, "but I will need to do it again once or twice before the night is over, and then you have to take it off."

"Once or twice more? Really? But then isn't it hard to get any rest."

By now, Leon's member had been too hard for so long it shriveled up to nothing. "Well, darling, perhaps we should forget about marital relations for now; just hold each other and go to sleep."

"If you say so. May I please have my nightgown back?"

Leon rolled out of bed and handed her the nightgown. "I'll be in the other room," he said. "Go to sleep".

Leon sat and morosely stared at the dying embers. *Well, Lord, you got me into this mess. I could use some help here.* "You are doing fine. Just take one step at a time. Try again in the morning".

Thus ended their wedding night.

***

Next morning the sun had been up for hours when Leon awoke to the sounds of retching coming from the closet. *Oh, no! Esther!* The whole miserable night came back to him in a flood. He leaped out of bed and rushed to her side. He grasped her body. Esther shook her head. Between gags she gasped, "Don't touch me."

He stood by, feeling completely useless. "Darling what can I do to help?"

"Cool cloth," she choked.

Leon hurried to wring out a cloth in the tepid wash water. "Here's the cloth." He held it out to her and she pointed to her face. Leon held the cloth to her forehead. It seemed to quiet her. She was covered in sweat. He wiped her face. "Can you make it back to the bed?" She nodded. "Here let me help you up." He steadied her as she stumbled into bed. "Is it like this every morning?"

She nodded, sank back into the pillows and covered her face. Leon perched on the edge of the bed and watched her. Several minutes later she began to breathe steadily. "Will you be all right, now?" He inquired.

"Yes, I think so," she replied. "You may go down and have some breakfast. I will rest a while. Just bring me up some dry toast and tea when you come back."

"All right, darling, if you're sure."

***

The trip home from Lansing seemed to drag. Leon had dismissed his driver as he preferred to take the reins himself. Esther rode alone in the carriage, unhappy but relieved the whole thing was over.

Back home at last, Leon helped her into the house, paid his respects to her mother and excused himself as soon as propriety allowed. "Esther is a bit tuckered out this morning. If you don't need me for anything, I think it best if I go over to the farm and get some work done."

"No problem. I will make sure Esther gets some rest. Then she can tell me all about the wedding. Will you be back for supper?"

"Yes, I will see you later. Have a good day, Millie."

***

CHAPTER EIGHTEEN – Esther's Confinement

The month of December had dragged by in a fog. It was now well into the month of January, the dead of winter in Michigan. Esther's morning sickness had lessened somewhat. Her belly was beginning to pooch out and tiny flutters had started in her womb. It was amazing how she knew the first time it happened what those flutters were.

Leon was spending more and more time away from her. The snow was heavy this time of year. Leon had to keep the paths open, water and feed the animals and exercise the horses. Sometimes he missed his old gang, but he wasn't tempted to resume those relationships. He heard Winifred had a new boyfriend.

Often times he didn't return to Esther until almost bedtime. She greeted him upon his return but rarely smiled. Leon enjoyed spending a few minutes with Walter and Millie before the fire. He even tried taking up the pipe, but quickly realized it would never be his choice of activities.

His efforts at lovemaking with Esther had yet to produce results. Esther was stiff and unresponsive. She refused to get rid of the dreaded flannel nightgown, even during intercourse. Leon was barely able to mollify his own physical craving, and failed completely in arousing hers, much less satisfying her.

Doris and Bill were to be married in June. The construction of their house was underway. Doris spent as much time as she could over at her new house, helping Bill. Her close relationship with Esther had changed. They no longer spent hours talking and giggling far into the night. Doris had her own concerns now and Esther was not confiding hers. Doris was ashamed to admit she was somewhat embarrassed by Esther's condition. As time went on, she tended to doubt the story Esther had told, although she kept it to herself and Bill.

Millie suspected things were not going well between the newlyweds, but she did not want to interfere. Everything she had ever learned taught her it was up to the wife to make the marriage work.

96

She was chagrined to think her own daughter was falling short. One evening she voiced her concerns to her husband, "Walter?"

Walter put down his reading and bent to light his pipe. "Yes, Millie?"

"What do you make of our newlyweds?"

"What do you mean?"

"Well I… you know, I just don't see the sparks flying between them."

"I suppose you may be right."

"So, what do you think?"

"Can't say as I think anything."

"Surely you've noticed Leon is away over at the Hubbard farm almost all day, every day and Esther mopes and moves around the house like a mere wraith. She hardly gives me any help at all."

"I see," Walter puffed on his pipe and blew out a few smoke rings. "Hm, perhaps I will speak with her. You have every right to expect her to do her share. After all she is a married woman now and is eating at our table."

"No, Walter, you missed the point."

"I did?"

"The point is her and Leon. Things are not going well between them."

"Mm, I see." Walter picked up his book.

"Well, what should we do about it, Walter?"

"What do *you* think we should do?"

"If I knew I wouldn't be asking you!"

"Nothing."

"Nothing, what? Come on, Walter. Stop playing dumb. You are no good at it."

"Oops you caught me!" Walter grinned. "Well, here's the thing," he continued, "There is absolutely nothing we can do. They are married and they have to work it out for themselves, the same way we did and everyone else did. You can insist Esther grow up and take on her share of responsibilities around here, but so far as her relationship with Leon is concerned, it's their problem. You get involved at your own peril. No one really knows what goes on with another couple behind closed doors."

"I see," said Millie, although she wasn't sure she saw at all.

"You aren't sure, are you, dear? Well, my advice is to give it more time. It is always tough on newlyweds, living with their parents. Once they have the privacy of their own home, I'll wager things will improve. I'm not sure Esther feels very married, yet. She's had a lot to deal with. Leon is trying, but he is no God, either. I'm sure he won't give up. Give them time."

***

February and March blew by.

The spring thaw came, revealing the first crocuses poking up their heads. Esther's tummy was blossoming, as well. In addition, she was feeling lots better and had been helping Millie with chores without much encouragement. With the return of her appetite, Esther had all but taken over in the kitchen. Millie enjoyed teaching her as much as possible of her cooking techniques. Esther was making her own cookbook of treasured family recipes.

Evenings she joined her parents by the fire as she sat sewing garments for the new baby. Walter refurbished a family heirloom antique cradle and carved little toys and rattles for the baby in his woodworking shop. Esther had even started to laugh a little. Sometimes the three of them played a game around the fire and thought up silly names for the baby.

"My grandson will be called Morris Avis Douglas," Walter declared, "MAD for short."

"Not at all," said Millie. "My first granddaughter will be Beatrice Alice Douglas, BAD for short.

"You're both wrong," opined Esther, "My twin girls will be named Madeline and Bathsheba, Mad Bath for short."

Millie and Walter groaned in unison.

***

After the mud season was over and the ground had settled once more, Esther decided it was safe to venture away from the house. Otis had all but disappeared from her concerns. He stuck to the barn and rarely came near the house. Esther took to walking down the lane and back, a mile or two every day.

The married ladies of Millie's quilting circle all advised it. The fresh air and exercise were excellent preparation for the rigors of childbirth. Also, she must drink three glasses of milk a day and eat lots of meat, vegetables and fruits.

Once or twice the married ladies began to speculate on Esther's due date in relationship to her hasty wedding. Millie quashed the muttering immediately with her killing stare. No more mention was made.

Esther did her best to follow the health-giving routine. Her cheeks were rosy after coming in for her daily walk. "Hi, Mom, I'm back," she called out.

"In here, Esther," answered Millie. "I put on the tea kettle. Why don't you make two cups and we'll sit a spell?"

Esther prepared the tea and added two cookies to the saucers. "Here you go," said Esther, plopping her expanding behind into a rocker.

"How was your walk?" asked Millie.

"Same as always. Well, not really exactly the same. There is always something new to see, popping out of the ground, or some animal or bird passing through. I saw my first robin."

"Excellent!" opined Millie. "A sure sign spring is here to stay."

"You may be right. I had to remove my sweater half way through my walk. You know, there is one funny thing, though. Well, not funny. I mean strange."

"Oh?" Millie nibbled on a cookie.

"It seems odd Dad's hired hand is out with the cows. I see him almost every day. What do you suppose Father has him doing out there?" Esther sipped her tea.

"I don't know. I leave those things up to your father. Maybe one of the cows is lame, or about to give birth or something."

"Whatever. The man gives me the creeps. Maybe I will walk up the road tomorrow instead of down the lane."

"Fine. Just let me know which way you are going. I appreciate knowing where you are and watch out for those new-fangled motor cars tearing down the hill scaring the horses to death."

"I'll watch out, Mother," Esther chuckled.

Esther thought little more about Otis, although she was always careful to check her surroundings. One night she imagined she saw him staring in the window, but when she got up to look out, no one was there.

***

Walter was a respected member of the community. He was one of the elders in the church and served on the township council. As such, he was considered a confidant of the pastor, mayor, and local sheriff. After the council meeting, the mayor took Walter aside. "This is in complete confidence, Walter, you understand?"

"You have my word, of course, Dean, any time."

"Well, here's the thing, the sheriff and I are beginning to wonder if there isn't something to these stories we're hearing about the girl claiming she was attacked. At first we chalked it up to some loose girl making up a story to cover up her getting in a family way. You know it happens all the time, but three times in six months, in a town this size? Doesn't seem likely."

Walter's stomach did a flipflop. A frown crossed his face, "I guess I haven't heard those stories, Dean."

Herb, the local sheriff, joined them. Mayor Dean nodded to him, "I was just telling Walt our idea, Herb."

"Good plan," said Herb glancing at Walt, "I guess the mayor was wondering if you would support calling in the County on this one. I'm thinking maybe they would assign one of their investigators, undercover, of course, just to give me a little help, you understand?"

Dean explained, "We can cover the salary and expenses out of the regular budget for a while, but we may need a special appropriation eventually. We need to be careful to keep the girls' names out of this." He cleared his throat and tucked his thumbs into his belt. "I don't mind telling you one of these girls is the daughter of one of our finest families."

Oh God, what have I done? My failure to report Esther's attack has caused three more girls to meet the same fate. Lord only knows how many others. Walter swallowed hard. "Uh, you know I will support anything you need, Dean…Herb. Just say the word. Bring in this county investigator. The sooner, the better. We can't have our girls being attacked."

"Thank you for your support, Walter. I knew we could count on you. We need to get this guy before we have a local panic, you know what I mean?" said Dean, slapping Walter on the back.

"Right. Do what you need to do, men." Walter gave his hand to each one. "I'd best be shoving off."

"Goodnight, Walter. Say 'hello' to Millie for me."

"Sure, enough."

Walter rode home on his horse, Bess, mulling over the conversation. *What can I do? Dean will bring in this investigator. Should I approach him? I really will not know who it is, will I? Dean and the mayor will keep this investigation well buttoned up. Should I try to pry a name out of Esther? No, I can't, without revealing to her about the other attacks. I'm sworn to secrecy. If I ever get my hands on the rapist, I swear I'll... Oh dear God!*

Walter arrived at the barn without coming to any conclusions. He handed off his horse to Otis with instructions to remove the bridle, rub her down and give her a few oats and fresh water before closing her stall.

"Yes sir, Boss." Otis idolized Walter and Walter knew it. Walter was the first adult in Otis's life to treat him with kindness. Otis was a willing worker, so long as you gave him explicit instructions every time. One could not depend on Otis to remember correctly from one time to the next.

***

CHAPTER NINETEEN – Childbirth

Esther was quite sure when the baby was due, right about June 26th, although first babies were known to come whenever they were darned good and ready. Esther had been feeling wonderfully well, lately. Her condition was readily apparent, of course. After all it wasn't easy to hide seven pounds, or so, of baby on a ninety-five pound woman.

Esther continued her daily walks trying to vary them from the roadway in either direction, or down the lane or across the fields and down around the lake. She hadn't been bothered by Otis again, although she made certain to carry a stout walking stick and took one of the barn dogs with her. She had noticed Otis lurking nearby, sometimes, when she went out to gather eggs or carry milk in from the milking parlor. If she caught him staring at her, he would quickly look away and pretend to be doing something else.

Esther was a good two months away from term when she first began having false labor contractions. Millie had warned her about these, and sure enough, they were exactly as described, not painful at all, just an involuntary tightening and release all over her belly. There was a name for this medical phenomenon Esther couldn't quite remember, Braxton Hicks, she thought named after the doctor who first identified them. She became so accustomed to the periodic tightening she hardly noticed it anymore.

Millie had instructed her about these spasms. They should gradually gain strength until the real labor commenced. So, Esther wasn't concerned while out walking in late April when one particularly strong one came upon her.

Esther paused in her walk until the contraction faded away. Five minutes later another one came. After it let up, Esther decided to turn back toward home. Halfway home another one came. *Oh dear, that pesky baby is pushing on my bladder, again. It feels like a little urine has escaped.* She quickened her steps.

Esther was turning into the yard when another one hit. This time it was accompanied by a gush of water between her legs and running down into her shoes and stockings. Esther cried out and leaned back against a tree. She held herself and looked down in dismay. She stood there catching her breath when another strong contraction came. This one was very different from the false labor. Esther curled up on the ground panting for a good three minutes until it stopped. *I don't think this is false labor. I've got to get in the house and call Mother. Maybe she will hear me now.*

Esther rolled up onto her knees, cupped her mouth and called, "Mother, help me. Mother! Help!"

Just then Otis glided out from behind a tree. *Oh my God, Otis!* "Is sumpin' wrong, Miz Esther?" He shuffled over to her.

"Help me get into the house, Otis."

"Yes'm Miz Esther," said Otis. He bent over and picked her up in his arms with ease.

"No, no, I can walk." She started to scream in hysterics as a new pain hit.

"I've got you Miz Esther. Don't scream." Esther clamped her mouth shut despite the pain wracking her body. She remembered all too well what Otis might do to her if she screamed. There was no time to be terrified as Otis half ran with her up the steps to the front door. He kicked the door with one foot and it sprang open.

"My stars! What are you doing with Esther? Put her down, Otis," screamed Millie. Otis lowered his arms and let Esther fall on the floor. Esther screamed in pain. Otis turned pale and ran out the door.

"Oh my darling! Oh, oh, oh, my poor baby, what is wrong, what did he do to you?" cried Millie. "Here, let me help you up."

"No, Mother," gasped Esther. "Just give me a minute. It's the baby. It's started. Otis was only helping me."

At last Millie took in the situation, the wet dirty pantaloons, stockings and skirt, the way she was holding her stomach. "Your water broke, didn't it?"

Esther nodded and caught her breath as the contraction lessened. "I think I can get up now if you will help me."

"Just let me put a cover on to protect the bed and then you can lay down right in our bedroom. Will you be okay for just a second?"

"Can you call for Doris?"

"No, she and Bill are off working on their house."

" Well…I'm okay for a minute or two…but hurry."

"I'll be right back." Millie sprang into action and whipped off the bedclothes, covered the mattress with a rubber sheet then an old but clean, blanket with a sheet on top. "Okay, we're ready. Let's get you settled."

Esther was grateful to lie down. She rolled over on one side and waited. Millie covered her with another clean sheet.

"I'm going to clean you up and get you into something more comfortable. I'll be right here in the kitchen if you need me." Millie set to work heating water for a bath and setting out clean night clothes for Esther. Esther called her twice during contractions. Millie rubbed her back and spoke quietly until they let up.

Walter came into the kitchen just as Millie walked in. He pulled out a chair and sat down at the table. "How's it going, babe?"

"Not so good, actually." Millie filled him in on what happened.

"This doesn't sound good for the baby, does it?"

"Not at all. Let's hope the pains go away. If they do, we must continue to keep her isolated and still for as long as we can. There is always the danger of infection once the water breaks."

"Should I send someone for another midwife or do you plan to deliver your own granddaughter?"

"Not yet, anyway. Let's just keep her quiet and see how she does. The baby is still way too early. Very few seven-month babies live, you know. They don't have the strength to nurse."

"I've raised enough tiny farm animals with an eyedropper to know how it goes. Should I go get Leon?"

"I don't know. He would just be another one to care for. Let's wait a little bit and see."

Just then Esther screamed, "Mom, Mother," sounding a bit desperate.

***

An hour later Millie had Esther washed and settled back down in a clean nightgown and fresh sheets. Her contractions hadn't gotten any harder. There was little to do but wait. Esther drifted off to sleep between contractions. She seemed to be more content when Millie stayed with her. Thus Millie made little progress on supper. She tried to ignore the rumblings in her stomach. *Maybe supper will just have to be a little late today.*

"Dinner is served," called a cheery voice as a cart rumbled across the floor. "Hello, ladies. I've got what you want," Walter sang out. He pushed the tea cart into the bedroom. It was loaded with plates, sandwiches, sauce dishes of fruit, cookies and beverages. "Here we are, ladies. People who are laboring need their sustenance."

"Oh, Daddy, this is fantastic!"

"Thank you, darling." Walter grinned and puffed out his chest. "I remind you, we men aren't totally worthless in the obstetrics ward."

"Yum, it looks delicious," Millie began to plump pillows and smooth covers. "Here, let's put some pillows behind her back so she can sit up and have a bite."

"Now, Millie, you have to promise that you won't expect this kind of special treatment all the time," Walter cautioned with a grin.

"Oh you dear sweet man!" Millie rewarded him with a kiss on the cheek. "Thank you. I was just thinking about how hungry I am. I hope you can sit down here and enjoy this with us."

Walter frowned as Esther experienced another contraction. Millie calmly removed her plate and began massaging Esther's back. "Don't hold your breath, honey; just breathe lightly through your mouth. Little breaths…good. No, don't curl up your pelvis. You don't want to bear down. We want to keep this baby in there as long as possible, don't we?"

Walter marveled at his wife's work, with love and admiration. He reflected on the miraculous way women have helped women give birth since time began. Soon the contraction subsided and everyone returned to normal. Millie handed Esther her plate and picked up her own sandwich, trying not to wolf it down.

"Hello, I'm home," sang out a male voice. "Where is everybody?"

"We're in the bedroom, Leon. Come on in."

Heavy boots walked in from the back door. "Well, hello you people. What's up with the wife? She looks a little pale."

"She has gone into early labor, Leon. We are just sitting with her having a bite to eat. We haven't had a chance to prepare a full supper but there are plenty of sandwiches here," Millie offered.

Leon grabbed a sandwich. Between bites he continued to ply Millie with questions. "I don't understand. What's going on here? Why is my wife in bed? Her baby isn't due yet." Leon reached out to his wife. "What are you doing in bed? Are you sick? On no, I hope it's not the influenza!"

"Calm down, Leon. She's not sick."

"I'm not sick, Leon. I was just out taking my daily walk and all of a sudden my water broke, so here I am," she managed a smile.

"Your water broke." he echoed.

Millie added, "She was just turning into the front yard, when her water broke, and Otis picked her up and carried her into the house. I

107

was in the dining room when he brought her right up the steps and kicked the door open."

"What!" Leon demanded. "You mean that filthy moron had his hands on my wife! What is going on here while I'm away trying to earn a living! What on earth are you doing, Esther, fooling around with a lowlife? I can't believe this!"

"You don't understaaa…Ohhh…" Just then Esther started another contraction. Leon continued waving his arms and stomping around in the adjoining dining room.

Millie tried to help Esther get through the contraction. She cast a pleading look at Walter who could do nothing but shrug his shoulders, gesture helplessly and mouth the words, "Who me?" Millie mouthed back, "Yes you," and gestured toward the door. Walter got up out of his chair, left the room and closed the door.

Leon whirled on him. "Now, I demand to know what is going on between my wife and your creepy farm hand! No wonder I can't get a rise out of her in bed. She's carrying on with … with … whatever!" He waved his arms wildly. "I can't believe this!" he continued.

Walter began, "Now, see here, Leon, there's no need to…"

"No need! How can you say no need? That's my wife in there!" He gestured wildly and headed toward the bedroom.

Walter grabbed Leon's arm, half pulled him out into the kitchen, and lowered his voice, "And my daughter, Leon."

Leon sank into a chair, held his head in his hands, elbows on his knees and slowly shook his head. "Oh, my God, dear God, how could you allow this to happen? I took her for my wife, Lord. How can this be? Oh, God," he moaned.

Walter saw a totally heartbroken man. He quietly closed the door, came up behind Leon and rested a hand on his shoulder. Walter breathed a prayer of his own. *Give me words to stop this bleeding soul, Lord.*

"Leon...son...you are the son of my heart whom I did not have of my own seed...listen to me...please listen. Son... I heard the same words you did. I heard what my wife said. But, Leon, she must have misspoken. We have to give her a chance to explain what happened.

"And we have to give Esther a chance to explain. I know for a fact Esther despises Otis. She is afraid of him. We can't assume she is having an affair with Otis just because of a few words Millie said."

"Everyone is under stress, here. There has to be an explanation. Now, I think you should just calm down until we have had a chance to question them. They are both in there and we will soon go in and find out the truth. And, one more thing, Leon, your wife is in labor. I've been watching her in labor for two hours now. We are very concerned about the baby. It is much too early for the baby to survive outside the womb."

Walter continued, "Esther's water did break, like she said. It was spontaneous. Nothing happened to cause it to break. Sometimes this happens. You've seen it with the farm animals. The baby is in danger, Leon. Now, please try to calm down. No matter what you think about this business with Otis, it is important for the sake of the baby you try not to upset Esther. Do you hear me? Do you understand?"

Leon raised his tear-filled eyes. "You are the Father I didn't have, too. Thank you for talking some sense into me. I jumped to conclusions and went crazy. I'm sorry, Walter. Please, forgive me."

"Of course I forgive you. You have a legitimate concern. I don't like it a bit better than you do. We'll get to the bottom of this, in due course but first things first. For now, Esther and the baby are our foremost concerns.

"Before I drop this discussion, I didn't fail to notice your remark about your wife's treatment of you in bed. Leon, I'm glad you let it slip, because it will not be tolerated, not one bit. There are several things which have to be brought out into the open here, but like I said, first things first."

Leon only looked down in embarrassment.

Walter sat down at the table and lit his pipe.

It would be many hours before Walter and Leon would be able to get to the bottom of the incident about Otis carrying Esther. As is the fate of all fathers-to-be, they were assigned the difficult task of waiting while mysterious sounds came from the birthing room, or even worse, no sound at all for long minutes.

From time to time Millie took a kitchen break. At those times she gave a report to the weary men who kept vigil at the coffee pot.

Unfortunately, she was unable to shed any more light on the Otis situation. "I didn't see a thing until the door burst open and there was Otis carrying Esther. She was silent but obviously she was a mess. I made a mistake. You know how Otis is about instantly following orders to the letter without using any common sense. I almost screamed at him, 'Otis, what are you doing? Let go of her' and he instantly dropped his arms and let her fall right to the floor. Then he turned and ran out of the door and disappeared.

"She wasn't seriously hurt, but she felt the pain. Do you want me to ask her how Otis happened to have her? I don't want to upset her, but maybe I can say something."

"Don't upset her," said Leon. "There'll be time to ask her later."

"Well, I'm sure he didn't do anything to cause this. But…oh…now I remember. She did say something… Let me think…I think I said something to her like 'What did Otis do to you? Did he hurt you?' and she said 'No, Mother, Otis was just helping me'. Yes, I'm sure she said, 'Otis was just helping me' right after he ran out." Millie paused and looked at them both.

Leon sat back, drew in a deep breath and blew it out. "What a relief! I'm so glad you remembered." Leon slowly shook his head, "I should have known."

"Yes, Millie, it's a good thing you remembered," said Walter, "but we still need to get the whole story from Esther as soon as she is up to it and the baby is out of danger."

"I understand," said Millie. "Well, I need to get back in there. Maybe you men ought to try to get some sleep. This could take some time, you know, and I will call you if anything happens."

"What do you think, Walter, do you want to go upstairs and stretch out?" asked Leon.

"You know, son, I've been through this a time or two. I reckon I might just take her advice."

"I think I will stick around here a little while," said Leon. "I'll probably be up later if nothing happens."

***

Leon had fallen asleep at the table, his head cradled in his arms. Walter had passed out upstairs on a bed. Millie was dozing in her chair beside Esther whose contractions seemed to have stopped. Doris had come home and was asleep in her room. As dawn crept silently through the trees, the crisis seemed to be over. Leon was the first to awaken, his muscles and joints protesting. Falling asleep at the kitchen table did not serve the body well. Leon stretched and slowly shuffled across the kitchen to poke up the coals in the iron stove, get the fire going and set the coffee on to boil. Before long, it was perking merrily away.

Leon went downstairs to the cellar where he performed a similar task in the wood furnace. Soon heat was pouring out and up the bonnet above the furnace and through the large square register in the dining room floor. Returning up from the cellar, he tiptoed to the bedroom door to peek in. Both women were sleeping peacefully, a very good sign. Relieved at the sight, he returned to the kitchen to pour his morning cup of coffee.

Stirring sugar and cream into the coffee, Leon offered up his morning prayers, full of thanksgivings and petitions. He looked up as Walter entered the room, tucking in his shirt. "Morning, Walter."

"Morning, Leon. I see the girls are both zonked out. Must be things have settled down."

"Yes, I've not heard a sound from their direction. I guess the baby is going to survive another day, thank the Lord. Coffee?"

"Right you are. Gotta get the eyes open, you know."

"Assuming Esther's contractions have stopped, where do we go from here?"

"Well, I figure Millie will have her hands full waiting on Esther. You and I will need to keep our respective farms going, take care of the livestock, and do what we can to help Millie."

"Sounds like a good plan. Let's fix breakfast here. Then we can head on out."

"Did someone mention breakfast?" Millie entered the kitchen looking as if she had slept in her clothes.

"Sit right down and make yourself comfortable. One coffee coming right up," said Leon.

"Any news from the infirmary?" asked Walter. He pulled out a half-dozen eggs and started cracking them into a bowl, as Leon sliced strips of bacon and laid them in a pan.

"Well, the contractions slowed down and stopped half way through the night so we were both able to sleep. I expect Esther to sleep for several hours, now."

The bacon sizzled in a large iron skillet. Leon flipped it over once, put a dollop of butter to melt in another pan while he whipped up the eggs with a fork and started some fried toast in a third pan. Walter pumped enough water to fill the reservoir attached to the stove for hot water. He put three plates in the warming oven.

Walter took a seat next to Millie, "Did you learn any more about the Otis deal?"

"No, I didn't ask, but I can assure you Esther does not like Otis. She's afraid of him. A few days ago she mentioned seeing him watching her when she was out walking. The next day she started walking up the road instead of in the lane. Also, she started carrying a stout stick and taking one of the dogs with her."

112

"I wish I had known about this," said Walter, glancing at his wife. He finished up his coffee and rose to fill the cups.

"Breakfast is ready, folks," said Leon as he divided the bacon and eggs onto three plates and added toast on the side. He saved some toast in case Esther woke up hungry.

Walter gave thanks for the food and they bent to their tasks. "Excellent food, Leon," said Walter.

"Yes, it is," said Millie. "Correction, yes it was. I ate the whole thing and I'm stuffed."

"Well, I'd better get started," said Walter.

Just then a yell came from the bedroom, "Mom...Mo---other!"

Three pairs of feet hit the floor running. Millie arrived first and went immediately to Esther's bedside. "What is it?"

"The c-c-cramps are back."

"Is this the first one?"

"Y-yes. I feel like pushing, Mom."

"Just relax and try not to push. Pant like a dog. There, much better." Millie took charge of the situation. "Walter, I'll need you and Leon to help. You fetch me my midwife birthing kit. Leon, you go out to the kitchen and bring hot water, a basin, plenty of towels. Hurry."

The men leaped to their assigned tasks, relieved to have something useful to do. Millie put the bedpan under Esther. "Can you go a little bit for me?"

Millie proceeded to don a surgical gown and mask and scrub her hands and arms. She shaved and washed Esther and turned to scrub again.

By now the men had returned. "Now what?"

"Leon, please remove Esther's bed pan and then cover her a bit with one of those clean towels."

"Consider it done."

"Now, gentlemen, please watch me scrub up with this disinfecting soap and then you do the same."

They moved to follow instructions. "Good job," said Millie.

"Now you men can help me turn Esther sideways across the bed and place several pillows under her back, head, and shoulders. We'll need a chair on each side. Leon you sit in the chair at the head and hold your wife up on the pillows. Your job is to hold her, talk quietly to her and encourage her."

Millie placed several clean towels under Esther and covered her with a clean sheet. "Walter, please get out a couple of the flannel receiving blankets for the baby and lay them beside Esther. Just hold them by the edges. Thank you. We want to keep everything as clean as possible to prevent infection. Good job, everybody. Now, Esther, let's deliver this baby. Take a deep breath."

Esther's belly began contracting again.

"It's all right to bear down now," Millie instructed.

Esther made a high-pitched sound as she strained.

"Okay Esther, you can relax for a minute, now." Millie kept her hand on Esther's stomach so she could anticipate the next contraction.

"Here it comes again. Get ready to push. Take a deep breath. Very good, you're doing great. I see a little something. Probably the baby's head is starting to come. Next time we will make some real progress.

"Here we go again. Ah, I see the baby's butt. You can relax a minute, Esther. We don't want to deliver the baby butt first. There are a couple of things we can try. Sometimes it is possible to turn him around." Using her hands on Esther's stomach, Millie tried to turn the baby.

Esther screamed, "Noooo!"

Millie stopped immediately. "All right. That's too painful. We will just pull his little feet down and bring the baby out feet first. This will hurt some, Esther." Millie reached in a finger, hooked a rubbery little leg and popped it out like a cork. Esther yelped. "I'm sorry I had to hurt you. One more time. I'll make it quick." Millie popped the other leg out before Esther could draw breath to yelp again. "Ah, now we've got you, Baby. I've got both his little tootsies right here in my hand. One more good push Esther and we'll have this baby out of there. Here it comes. Big breath. Push hard, honey. Keep pushing. Here he comes. Ah, gotcha'! Will you just lookie here at what you've got – a beautiful baby girl! Well, she's not too pretty just yet, but we will fix her right up," Millie grinned, oblivious of the sweat on her brow. "Hello, there, Baby, welcome to the world," Millie said as she placed the baby onto the receiving blanket and started to clean her up. "Suction, please Walter." Walter handed her the rubber suction bulb from her midwife kit. Millie sucked mucus out of the mouth and nostrils. Millie held out her hand, "Scissors and string." Walter hand her the surgical scissors for cutting and tying off the umbilical cord.

The little girl started to cry and turned a pretty pink. "Well, now, I'm glad to hear you have a nice voice there, Baby." Everyone grinned, except Esther. Millie wrapped the baby and held her up for Walter to see. "Say hello to your grandfather, you sweet thing."

Millie offered the baby to Esther. Esther turned her head away. "I don't want her."

A shadow crossed Millie's face but she did not comment, instead she offered the baby to Leon. He took her with a look of awe and rapture on his face, cuddled her to his chest and began to coo to her. "Say hello to your papa, Little One."

Esther stiffened when he called the baby by an endearment reserved just for her. The baby quieted down. Leon walked out into the dining room, sat by the heat register and began to rock and sing nonsense to the baby.

Millie delivered the placenta, cleaned up Esther and gave her a fresh nightgown, pads and linens. She helped Esther move and settle on the bed then tiptoed out. Meanwhile Walter cleaned and repacked Millie's midwife supplies and cleaned up the mess of utensils and laundry.

When all was tidied, Millie and Walter settled wearily at the kitchen table. "Whew, not a bad day's work and it's only nine o'clock in the morning," said Walter.

"I wonder if there is any coffee left," said Millie, "But I'm too pooped to go check."

"I'll fix us some hot chocolate. That will be better for you." Walter rose to set some milk on to warm and mixed some cocoa and sugar together. "You were magnificent, Millie. I'm so glad I got a chance to see you in your work. It was fascinating."

"I'm glad you got to see it, too. Not every delivery gets this hairy, but generally a full-term baby takes longer to deliver. I've enjoyed my midwifery profession for how long, now? Three years?"

"It's been five years, honey," said Walter, pouring the hot chocolate into two mugs.

"Wow, time flies when you're having fun." Millie took a careful sip. "Just right. This is so good. Thank you, darling. I must say, I'm discovering a whole lot of new talents in you."

"I've got talents I haven't even used yet," said Walter with a twinkle.

"I think I will take you along as my assistant next time I go on a delivery. You were a big help."

"When it's your granddaughter being born, you have an incentive to do well. I'm not sure I want to take it up as a regular thing." Walter drained his cup and rose to get a refill.

"I wouldn't want to get you all tired out, dear. Who would I get to rub my back when I returned home?"

Walter chuckled, moved around behind Millie and started massaging her shoulders. "I can take a hint."

"Ah … Oooo … a little higher … there's the spot!" Millie squeaked. "Mm, don't quit."

"How about I take you upstairs and give you a real massage?"

"Later, dear, later," said Millie.

116

"Promises, promises," teased Walter as he moved back to his chair.

"You stopped!" protested Millie.

"Somehow I lost my incentive," he grinned.

"Men! They're all alike! One thing on their mind." laughed Millie.

"And it's a darned good thing, my dear, or you'd be out of a job," quipped Walter.

Leon walked into the room, carrying his new daughter.

"Have a chair, Daddy, and I'll pour you some hot chocolate," Walter offered.

"Thank you, hot chocolate sounds good," said Leon. "Hey, I like my new title, Daddy. What do you think, Little One? I'm your Daddy," he cooed to the baby.

"The man's hooked already," observed Millie.

"Yep, he's a 'goner' all right," Walter agreed. "You look natural, Leon, holding your tiny bundle."

"Millie," asked Leon, "May I ask you a question?"

"Certainly, what is it, dear?"

"Do all new mothers act like that when they deliver?"

"You mean the way she turned away from the baby?"

"Yeah."

"I've never seen it happen before. Hopefully, after she gets some rest she will respond to the baby. Truthfully, I was surprised."

"Should we be worried?"

"Yes, if it continues."

Walter observed, "I've seen it happen with animals, especially if there are multiple births. Sometimes first-time mothers will reject one of the babies. Oftentimes it will be the weakest one among them. Seems to be nature's way."

"What do you do?" asked Millie.

"Depends on how badly I want to keep the rejected one. Sometimes, I'll have an experienced mother that will adopt the little one. Other times I have to raise them, myself. It's a twenty-four-hour proposition. Sometimes I just let them sink or swim on their own. However, if it is a prize race colt with superior bloodlines, I might hire a whole crew of people to feed the baby."

"We'll do that, if we need to," said Leon, giving his baby a kiss. "This one is too precious to let go. We'll do whatever it takes, won't we Little One?"

***

CHAPTER TWENTY – Baby Douglas

"Hello there, little mother, you're awake." Millie put on her best face and breezed into Esther's bedroom. "How are we feeling?"

"A little sore," whispered Esther. She cleared her throat. "What time is it, Mom?"

"A little after noon. Are you ready to sit up and have something to eat?"

"I'm starved."

"Speaking of starved, your daughter has been waiting patiently to meet her mother. I think she might nurse a bit. It would be good for both of you."

"I don't want her, Mother. Give her to the orphanage."

"Oh, Esther, you can't mean that."

"Maybe they will have some childless couples who want her."

"But, darling…"

"I've thought about this a long time, Mother."

"Leon loves her, already."

"Leon shouldn't have to raise a freak."

"But she's perfect! How can you call her a freak, Esther?"

"Easy. I know her father, her real father."

Millie fell silent.

"Leon must have strong, healthy, beautiful babies of his own. I won't saddle him with a monster."

"You can't be sure Esther," Millie argued.

"I'm sure."

"Well, at the very least we need to put the baby to your breast. Otherwise, she'll die."

"That would be a blessing."

"Esther Elizabeth, you can't mean it! Have some compassion! The child is innocent."

Esther rolled onto her side and turned her face away. "Bring it here."

Millie put the baby to Esther's breast every hour for the next two days. She stroked her cheek, helped the nipple into her little mouth and taught Esther how to cuddle her. Nothing worked. Esther refused to look at the baby and the baby did not have a strong sucking instinct.

Millie became more and more desperate. She sent Walter into town to search for a nursing mother who would donate some milk. Unbelievably there were none to be found. Walter rode into the county offices to speak with the clinic people. They promised to ship some mother's milk, but it would take a few days.

In the meantime, Millie warmed some goat's milk and fed it to the baby with an eyedropper. At least the baby could swallow. Millie, Walter and Leon set up a schedule of feedings round the clock. Each took a turn at night. Leon continued to hold and rock the baby while he sang to her. Millie pleaded with him to lay her down for a couple hours and get some rest. Leon could hardly bear to part with her.

At last the mother's milk arrived and the weary adults took heart. Maybe they finally had the magic potion needed to revive the baby. If they could keep her alive for just a few more weeks, she would begin to suck on her own.

Esther was up and around more each day but showed no interest in the little girl's struggle for life. Indeed, she took little notice of Leon or the baby. On the fourth day, she ascended the stairs and spent the remaining hours in her own room.

Leon had sent word to his farm employees to take over his duties for a few days. Still, he needed to get over there and check on things, if only for a couple of hours. Millie and Walter stayed with the baby, "We won't leave her alone for even one minute," Millie promised.

"I'll be back as soon as I can." Leon went out the door, stuffing his hat on and buttoning his coat on the fly.

Walter sat by the warm air register, rocking the baby. Millie joined him and sank wearily into a nearby chair. "Well, what do you think?" asked Walter.

"It will take a miracle." Millie shook her head.

"Miracles do happen," said Walter.

"We need a miracle, not just for the baby, but for our daughter's marriage, as well."

"I hear you," Walter pursed his lips and sighed.

They sat together in companionable silence, letting the tiredness drain from their bodies. The only sound was the rhythmic squeak of the rocking chair.

***

After five days of heroic struggle, Baby Douglas gave up her fight. She no longer swallowed the precious mother's milk. It drained out the sides of her mouth down her cheek wetting her little blanket. Her breathing became shallow, her body limp and still. Her passing was so quiet it was impossible to tell when life had ended. Leon held her for the longest time while silent tears ran down his face.

Walter went out to the woodworking shed to craft a miniature coffin. He brought it into the house and Millie lined it with a soft new baby blanket she had sewn, herself. When everything was ready, they brought the box into the dining room. "What do you think, Leon, will this be all right for burying the baby?"

Leon looked up with pain-filled eyes, "Thank you, Millie and Walter, too. It's just right for her."

Walter came in with arms laden with outerwear for everyone. "Shall we go?"

Leon kissed his baby, ever so gently, "Farewell, my Sweet." He lowered her into the box and softly closed the cover.

Walter helped him on with his jacket. "Will Esther go with us?"

Leon shook his head. The three of them turned and went out the back door of the kitchen. Leon carried the box containing his daughter's remains. Walter picked up two shovels he had placed there and followed Leon. Leon led them through the trees and up a knoll to a small clearing. He set the box down, held out his hand for a shovel, selected a spot and began to dig.

The two men worked in tandem and soon a deep hole had been dug. Walter and Leon removed their belts and placed the straps under the box. Holding onto the ends, the men lowered the box into the hole and pulled out the straps. The three of them circled the grave.

Millie took a small prayer book out of her pocket and began to read from the service for the dead, "Heavenly Father, Thou who art the giver and sustainer of all life, we bring this innocent babe into your keeping and pray a legion of angels to carry her soul into your loving arms so she may rest and abide with you until we can all be reunited together in heaven.

"Send your Holy Spirit, O Lord to comfort the hearts of those who are grieving, to wipe away every tear. Lord, it is not our privilege to understand your ways. We pray your love will sustain us in our time of grieving and will fill us with renewed hope and trust in You. Until the final trumpet calls us all to your side, we commit her body to the earth and her soul to you...Amen."

Walter and Leon began filling the hole with shovels full of earth. Millie set to work gathering dried grasses and wildflowers. When finished, they patted it down and covered the fresh grave with the dried wildflowers.

"You two go on home," said Leon. "I'll stay here a while longer. If you don't mind, Walter, I'd like to take advantage of your woodworking shop tomorrow to make a marker for her grave."

"We'd be honored," replied Walter.

Millie turned around and looked back just once. Leon's bent body stood silhouetted against the gray sky, his head bowed in grief.

***

122

CHAPTER TWENTY-ONE –Post Partum Depression

Leon felt numb. He went about his chores at the farm, but his heart wasn't in it. In just a few days the tiny girl had wrapped herself around his heart. Perhaps now was a bad time to be making any important decisions, but he knew he would have to confront some issues soon. Foremost among them was his relationship with his wife. Esther's behavior over the baby puzzled him. Something beyond his comprehension was going on. Leon knew he was being tested, but why? *Maybe if I knew the answer I could begin to get a handle on my situation. Oh well, one step at a time,* he thought, as he forked hay into the horse's stanchions and spread straw in their stalls. *Sometimes you just have to hang on and keep moving blindly forward.*

Lord, I thought I was answering your call to marry Esther. It seemed so clear to me at the time, but now I'm confused. Maybe I'm done. Is it over, Lord? Have I completed your call? Leon wondered if his mission was completed since the baby was dead. *I loved my baby, Lord. I loved Esther, too, but clearly she never loved me. She doesn't really need me anymore does she, Lord? Does it mean I'm free?*

It was clear Esther was not in love with him. He knew he had done his best and had given her all the love he could, but she did not, or could not return his love.

Leon finished caring for his horses and moved on to the sheep shed. As he mechanically spread food and cleaned pens, his thoughts turned toward his old girlfriend, Winifred. *I have no idea what Winifred is doing, now. She's probably moved on. Wouldn't take her long to find a new beau,* he thought wryly. Leon had completely cut himself off from his old gang.

By the time he had finished casting grain for the chickens and gathering eggs, Leon had made up his mind. For the time being, he decided to move back into his rooms at the Hubbard farm. Esther would be infirm for a few weeks. As she recovered from childbirth, Millie would care for her. *I guess all I can do is keep my options open and see what happens. I'm here, Lord, when you need me.* He would give both Esther and himself some time to recover. *I'll stay away from intimacy, for now,* he thought, with a sigh. He would not bed Esther again until he was certain of their future together.

    ***

Leon knocked twice and walked into the kitchen where Millie and Walter were having coffee. "Hello, Millie, Walter."

"Come in, Leon. Can I pour you some coffee?"

"Thank you, just a half cup, please."

"If I haven't said it before, Leon, you know we are so sorry you lost the baby," said Walter.

"Thank you, kindly. I can't thank you enough for your care of us. You two were just great. I am very grateful for everything, the way you delivered the baby, Millie, the little toys and casket you made, Walter, working to save her life and standing by me when we buried her. I can't thank you enough."

"You're welcome, son, that's what families are for."

"I'm going to go in and see Esther for a few minutes before I leave, and then I'm going to go back over to the farm. I'll be staying there at night for the time being. I will try to ride over once a day to check in with Esther."

Millie and Walter exchanged glances. There was an awkward silence. Leon looked down, twirled the hat in his hands and cleared his throat.

"Thanks for the coffee and everything. I'll be leaving after I see Esther."

Leon knocked softly and opened the door to Esther's room. She was lying quite still on the bed staring at the ceiling. "May I come in for a minute?"

Esther turned toward Leon and their eyes met.

"How are you feeling, Esther? Is the pain bad?"

"Not so much today."

"I see, very good. Are you getting your appetite back?"

"Some."

"You need to eat to get your strength back, and drink plenty of liquids too."

"I'll try."

"We buried the baby up in a pretty little clearing in among the trees on a little knoll. I'm going to build a cross in Walter's workshop to mark the grave tomorrow. I was wondering, Esther," he cleared his throat, "What name you would like to give the baby? I'll carve it on the cross."

"Nothing."

"What did you say?"

"Nothing, Leon, nothing."

"You want to name the baby Nothing?"

"No. I mean I don't want to name the baby."

"She was our little girl. We should give her a name."

"Not your little girl, Leon. Not my little girl. She was the spawn of an evil monster. I'm glad she's dead."

"But we put her in a little casket. Your father made the casket with his own hands and your mother made the little blanket to put around her. I held her in my arms. I fed her. I watched her die. She was innocent, a real person. She deserves to have a name Esther."

"No name, Leon, no name." Esther turned her face away and closed her eyes.

126

Leon stood by her bed silently for a few minutes. Then he bent his head, turned and slowly moved away, as rejected as the baby.

***

Working on the baby's cross brought Leon a measure of comfort. He hadn't slept much the previous night. As he shaped the pieces of wood, a kaleidoscope of memories of the last few days played through his mind.

What name should I give baby? The perfect name just wouldn't come. *Have faith,* he thought. You will know the name when you need it.

What name could I give someone so pure, so innocent? Someone who had three strikes against her before she even drew breath. She was such a tiny baby. The only thing we called her was baby. For five days and five nights, just baby girl. That's it! Baby. Baby Girl Douglas. Her name would be Baby Girl Douglas, because she was his baby and would be forever.

Leon bent to his task. He carved the name Baby Girl Douglas and the dates into the wood. Then he carefully filled it in with black paint, edged in pink and decorated with tiny rosebuds. When the paint dried he took a spade and sledge hammer and trudged up the hill again to the grave.

When he reached the grave he began to hum and talk to her as if she could hear him. *"Hi, Little One. I'm back. I brought you a nice marker for your resting place. How do you like the name I carved on it? Baby. Baby Girl Douglas. Douglas is my name, you see, and you are my baby girl. Forever. I'll miss you, sweetheart until we meet again, someday."*

Funny thing, I don't remember putting these flowers here yesterday. Maybe Millie and Walter were up here earlier. I wouldn't be surprised. Leon finished up his work, stood in silence for a while and left.

***

It had been three weeks since Esther rid herself of the awful thing growing in her. She was up and dressed every day now and joining her parents for meals. Too late, Esther's milk had come in, which caused some discomfort. Millie treated her breasts with warm oil, three times a day to soften the lumps and prevent sores. Each time she wrapped Esther's breasts, tightly, to block some of the milk production. Gradually the breasts returned to normal.

There had been a few callers. Most of them were Millie's friends who came to pay respects. The conversation was strained and awkward and the visitors did not stay long.

Leon stopped by every day at different times. Esther never knew when to expect him. When he came the two of them visited for a few minutes about the farm or the weather then ran out of things to say. Leon excused himself to go up the hill and visit the grave for a half hour or longer. *Apparently he had more to say to a horrible dead fetus than he had to say to me, his living and breathing wife,* thought Esther.

Sometimes Esther wondered why the Lord hadn't taken her instead of the baby. *Surely, Leon would have been happier.* Clearly, Leon had never loved her. *I'm not even sure why he married me, perhaps through some misguided sense of honor.* Esther felt useless and unhappy.

Worst of all was the sense of guilt. *I'm of no use to anyone.* She was shamed forever by what she had done, going off to town with a rapist. *It didn't matter what Mother said.* Esther knew in her heart she should never have gone. *I sensed at the time Otis was evil.* She should have acted out of her own intuition.

I could have made some excuse, pretended I had a sore throat. No one should sing with a sore throat. Mrs. Lewis said so herself. It puts too much stress on the vocal folds. Yes, it would have been easy to make an excuse, without any hurt feelings. *If only...*

Esther was secretly relieved Leon was not spending the nights with her, relieved from the constant pressure to pretend something which wasn't there. They had not discussed it, but she appreciated the time off from her marital duties. Leon was gentle but the sexual act left her feeling nothing more than thankful it was over. She didn't mind the cuddling, but it was spoiled by the knowledge it always led to Leon taking his marital rights. It took away some of the joy.

Leon was so much larger than she, sometimes she was afraid of being smothered. He tried very hard to be considerate and not let his weight crush her, but she felt she had to brace herself to keep it from happening. Leon was not a heavyweight, simply tall and all muscle.

***

Springtime had arrived. The middle of May was a busy time on the farm and Esther's favorite time of year. The birds returned from their winter sanctuaries, mated and built their nests. Spring flowers bloomed and trees came to life. Warm and sunny days encouraged long walks and time spent out-of-doors simply observing all the activity. Cool nights kept the mosquito population down.

By all rights the change of season should have lightened Esther's mood. Perhaps it did to some extent, but she still found her thoughts drifted to suicide from time to time. She realized, however, suicide would be a cowardly act. It would solve her problems but at a tremendous cost to her parents. Besides, wishing it were so wouldn't make it happen. She had no idea how to go about killing herself.

As May drifted into June, Esther saw less and less of the men in her life. The lengthening hours of daylight required them to spend long days in the fields. Millie, too, was busy as she planted her huge garden, kept up with church activities, and delivered babies. Esther's options were limited. She certainly had no interest in witnessing another childbirth.

Sometimes she went along with Mother to her church groups. Although they were seldom unkind, Esther could not help but feel out of place among women twice her age. Their poorly disguised inquiries into the timing and circumstances surrounding her pregnancy and the death of her baby, made her exceedingly uncomfortable.

Likewise, she gave no thought to joining in a group of young married women. All they talked about was their babies and husbands. They all pretended to be so disgustingly happy, Esther wanted to throw up.

***

CHAPTER TWENTY-TWO – The Showdown

It was June twenty-sixth. She should have been giving birth on this very day. Instead, she was bending over a row of carrots, removing the weeds and thinning out the weakest of the seedlings to make room for the others to grow. Only ten o'clock in the morning and she was already bathed in sweat. This was going to be a hot one. It was good to get an early start on the outside work so she could work inside during the hottest hours of the day. She was grateful for the activity. It kept her mind from drifting in unwanted directions.

A shadow fell across her vision. A deep voice startled her, "Esther."

"Oh!" She looked up at a shadowed face. The sun hung bright behind Leon's head and blinded her for a second.

"It's time," he said, "It's time we talked."

Esther rose to her feet and pressed a hand into her cramped back. She squinted at him, her face revealing nothing.

"We need to talk about…about us," he hesitated. "What is going to become of us?"

"I see," she said.

"I brought some lemonade," he offered. "Is there someplace shady where we can sit and talk?"

"Over here, I guess." She motioned toward a shady bench. "We can sit here and watch the garden grow."

Esther sat first and took a long swallow. "This tastes good. I was thirsty."

Leon joined her. "I thought you might be ready for a break."

"I was thinking about a short rest, just now."

"Then my timing was excellent. Speaking of timing, Esther, I've been doing some thinking. Seems to me it's time we talked things out."

"What do you want me to say, Leon?"

"Just the truth, Esther. We need to face the truth."

"I see."

"I've missed you, Esther. I miss being with you, feeling your soft body next to mine. Have you missed me, Esther? Even a little bit?"

"Truth?"

"Yes, truth."

"This is hard, Leon. I'm not sure I know the truth. In some ways I have enjoyed the last two months. It was so good to get rid of …of …you know." She stroked her belly. "There were times when I thought of you. We had some good times, riding out in the buggy, going on a picnic, but so many of the memories hurt. I'm trying to forget."

"What about the wedding?"

"It's a good memory, Leon."

"And the wedding night?"

"Horrible! Oh, I'm sorry. I shouldn't have said..." She covered her mouth and looked away.

"Yes, you should have. I guessed as much. It's important for us to be honest with each other, Esther. None of the nights were good for you, were they?"

Tears started to form in Esther's eyes, threatening to spill over.

Leon wiped a tear away. "Not so good, huh?"

She couldn't hold his steady gaze. The tears flowed harder. She sniffed and tried to stop them.

"It's all right, Little One, let it out." He offered his shoulder. She leaned into his chest and cried into his shirt.

"You called her 'Little One' too," she sobbed.

"Yes, I know. It bothered you, didn't it? But Baby came from you. I loved her, same as you, so I called her 'Little One.' One of our

132

problems is I can't understand why you couldn't love her. I'm glad you have told me how you felt. You are my only Little One now."

"I know it was unreasonable and childish of me to feel upset. I just couldn't stand hearing you call the baby by my special name, Little One."

"It's all right for you to feel something. We can't control our feelings. But we can try to recognize them and direct them elsewhere or just let them go. The worst thing is to bury them, Little One." He gave her a squeeze and looked down at her. "You are my Little One." He smiled at her.

"She pulled back and looked up into his eyes. You're right. I *was* feeling jealous and guilty. I'm so mixed up." She gave one last sniff, turned around and settled against the back of the bench. She picked up her lemonade. "I'd better drink this before it gets warm."

"It seems we have fixed one of our problems. From now on, you are my only Little One until we have a daughter of our own and you tell me it's all right to have two Little Ones."

"I'm not so sure, Leon."

"About what?"

"About our having a daughter or a son either."

"What do you mean?"

"Leon, I don't know exactly why you married me, but whatever it was, the reason is gone now. I want you to know I am willing to give you your freedom. You can go. You can marry anyone you want, Winifred, or whoever."

Leon was stunned. "I don't want to marry someone else, not Winifred, not anybody! I am perfectly happy with the wife I have already. We just have to work a few things out."

"There's more than a *few* things and not all of them are workable."

"Like what? Name one thing." He baited her.

"Well, I'm twelve years younger than you."

"Not a problem," dismissed Leon.

"It is for *me* and our age difference isn't going to change."

"It has already changed. You are not a little girl any more. You are a grown woman, who has been through marriage, gestation, childbirth and death. I don't think you would be happy with one of those young pups who were in your circle of admirers in high school."

Esther thought for a minute. "I suppose not."

"Whew, I'm relieved to hear you say so," Leon grinned.

She turned away to hide her corresponding grin. "Just don't get your hopes up too far," she teased.

"There's my girl again! You're getting your sense of humor back. When did we stop laughing at life?"

"Months ago."

"Yeah. Well, there's two down. Name another problem, if you dare," he challenged.

"All right, you asked for it, it's the same one that happens when we are sleeping together, every night about ten o'clock."

"Ouch! All right, this is the biggie. Our sex life hasn't rung any bells, has it?"

Esther nodded, morosely, and looked down at her hands.

"First, let me say this, Esther. I know it can be better. I know it *should* be better, especially between two people who care for each other. I'm not saying the people have to be in *love*. But, they have to be in accord and truly care for one another. Deep abiding marital love can grow from a good sex life and vice versa. They go together like milk and cookies, peaches and cream. A good sex life can bring harmony to a marriage. Without it, a marriage can grow cold."

"But, do you really think our problem was just…you know?"

"Yes, I think it is an important factor, but it is also possible our lukewarm sex life was more a symptom of some deeper problem, rather than the origin of our separation troubles. Perhaps we were hiding things from each other, keeping too much inside."

"So what do you suggest, Dr. D?"

"Well, our problems won't cure themselves overnight. I have some ideas, but it all depends on whether we like each other well enough to try again. We both have to agree to work at it. What do you think, Esther? Am I repulsive to you? Am I the man you want?"

"You are a wonderful man Leon, more wonderful than I can say. I am the weak one, here. I am so undeserving of you."

"Thank you, Esther. So, honey, are you willing to try again? Are you giving me a yes?"

She nodded, "Yes."

"Oh, this is so good! Come here, Little One." Leon held her for a long time. "From now on, we need to do this right. You need and deserve a courtship done the right way. I'm going to take you out. We'll do all the good things together, picnics, dancing under the stars, holding hands. I will bring you flowers and little gifts. I will kiss you and hold you, but we will not have sex, not until you beg me. You are going to climb all over me and demand I take you, understand?"

"Well, prepare yourself for a long wait."

"No problem. I've got lots of time. It will happen. Count on it. Until it happens, you will go on living here with your parents and I will stay in my room at Hubbard's. Now, I have a question for you."

"I'm listening."

With a grin, he removed his hat and placed it over his heart. "How about a date, Saturday night?"

"You're on."

"I'll pick you up at seven-thirty. Wear your dancing shoes."

"Right. Saturday night, seven-thirty, dancing shoes. Gotcha'"

"Goodbye, Little One." He dropped a kiss on her lips and almost ran for his horse.

Her heart did a little flip as she watched him go.

***

PART THREE

CHAPTER TWENTY-THREE – Courtship Done Right

"Your carriage awaits, madam," said Leon. A liveried coachman held open the door of a gleaming carriage. "You look so beautiful tonight darling," said Leon, "I love your dress."

"Thank you," she smiled shyly and fingered the tiny lace flowers on the off the shoulder neckline.

"What do you call the fabric? It looks special."

"It's only a lilac dimity," she demurred, as if she had not spent days getting ready for this evening.

"Ah of course, dimity, I should have known," he grinned. "Spin around for me please Sweetheart," suggested Leon. He watched the dress with approval as the skirt flared out from its high waist and fell in soft folds revealing her slim body. The silver buckles on her white dancing shoes flashed in his eyes. Leon nearly reached for her long shining hair as it swung out and settled again down her back.

Leon smiled mischievously, bowed, and whipped a small hand bouquet from behind his back. Esther peeked at him over the bouquet and noticed how handsome he looked in a dark blue suit coat with silver buttons, tailored gray slack trousers and a striped vest.

"Shall we?" he asked as he offered his arm. He helped her up into the carriage then jumped in beside her. Leon removed his roguish derby hat and set it on his knee.

"I have just the thing to finish off your outfit," said Leon. He reached into his pocket and brought out a gleaming necklace of pearls, faceted crystals and tiny lilac beads. "May I?" he asked and held it up to her neck.

"Oh Leon, it's perfectly beautiful. Thank you. I love it."

Leon fastened the necklace around her neck then leaned back to look at her, "Absolutely fetching." He slowly shook his head and with a twinkle in his eye said, "I'm sorry, Esther, something is still missing. Let me see, here." He reached in his other pocket and pulled out a matching dual stranded bracelet. "Ah, here we are. I think this may finish off the look." He held the bracelet around her wrist. "What do you think, darling? Shall we fasten this one, too?" Without waiting for an answer he hooked the bracelet around her wrist.

"Oh, I love it! You shouldn't have, but thank you, anyway!" She threw her arms around him and gave him a big kiss.

"Umm thank *you*!" After another kiss, he kept his arm around her and snuggled her up close. He knocked on the ceiling to signal the coachman to start. He smiled at Esther and gave her a kiss on the nose. "You smell wonderful, darling. I'm planning on having a great time tonight. I want to dance every dance with you."

Strains of music reached their ears as they neared the dance hall. Their carriage joined a line of others waiting to discharge their passengers. "Darling, look out this side at the view," suggested Leon.

She leaned into Leon to gasp at the dancing pavilion built on a forest of sturdy logs sunk deep into the lake bottom. Light blazing from every window joined with a full moon to gleam off the still waters of a Michigan lake. A porch, surrounding the building, was lit by a row of colorful Japanese lanterns.

Some guests arrived in boats which were tied up to the pier. The large parking area was nearly full of every kind of conveyance, from farm wagons to the new horseless carriages.

"Oh, this takes my breath away," said Esther as she gazed out the window. "Thank you for bringing me, Leon."

"How about if I claim my reward?" asked Leon.

"Why, kind sir, whatever could you possibly mean?" smirked Esther with a wide-eyed look and flutter of eyelashes.

"This," said Leon and pulled her into a kiss.

Esther wiggled her body around and fit herself into his arms. She felt herself giving way to his kisses, no longer stiff with fear. She pulled her lips away but remained in his arms. "May I speak the truth?"

"Yes, Esther, from now on, nothing but truth, the whole truth, between us."

"Well, please don't take offense. Promise?"

"Cross my heart and hope to die."

"It's just, I… I really like your kisses, and I like being close to you. You feel so good."

"How could I possibly be offended Esther sweetheart?" he spoke with his lips nearly touching hers. "You mean, like this, hmm?" He kissed her again.

"Well, this is hard to explain, but I like being able to just snuggle and kiss without having to worry about, you know, going all the way."

"You have my word. There will be no sexual relations between us until you say 'Yes' because *you* want them. You will never have to do it just to please your husband, understand?"

Esther visibly relaxed. She laid her head on his chest and sighed in contentment. "Just hold me Leon."

When it was their turn, the carriage pulled up to the boardwalk. The coachman leaped to open the door and assist Esther down. "Stay with the horses," Leon instructed. "I will send a boy when we are ready to leave." Leon offered his arm, "My lady?" They strolled off on a broad covered boardwalk connecting the pavilion to the mainland.

"I feel like a princess or something," smiled Esther. "Is this all a dream?"

"Oh yes, of course, it is the most delicious dream. You are certainly the most beautiful princess in all the lands and I am your Prince Charming."

Esther giggled and patted her hair, "But where is my diamond tiara, Sir?"

"I left it with the artisans at my diamond mine, Your Highness. I'm having it fitted with several more rows of diamonds."

"I want it now, right this minute." Esther pouted and stomped her dainty foot.

Leon roared with laughter. "You're very funny, Little One!"

They leaned over the railing to watch a family of ducks gliding by, the female duck was followed by a string of fuzzy little ones. The adult male brought up the rear. "Aren't the little ducklings adorable?" asked Esther. "I wish I had some bread to toss to them."

Leon watched her with amusement, "Those are wild birds, Esther. If it is ducks you like, I will buy you a duck farm."

"No need sir, the tiara will suffice, for now."

"You are so beautiful in the moonlight." Leon put his arm around her shoulders and smiled.

"I could stay right here," Esther sighed.

"Not for long I hope," said Leon. "You don't want to miss a chance to waltz with Prince Charming, do you?"

"Since you put it so modestly," said Esther, "Let's go in."

Leon turned and offered his arm, "I believe they are playing our song."

They entered a huge ballroom lit by four massive chandeliers set with hundreds of scented candles. At one end of the room a raised stage held a formally dressed society jazz band led by a slightly paunchy middle-aged conductor, well known in these parts. Leon took Esther in his arms and waltzed her into the line of dancers. Violins, trumpets, trombones and clarinets swelled with the strains of a Viennese waltz.

After a brief break the band swung into a new dance craze, the Foxtrot, named for the vaudeville performer, Harry Fox, who originated the dance. It soon spread across the country after he started it on the rooftop ballroom of the New York Theatre. Leon had practiced the complicated steps before he married Esther. "Shall we give this a try?" he asked.

"Oh, I don't know if I can. It looks rather difficult."

"We will start with a simple version." Leon backed up and pulled Esther along with him. "It takes a bit of practice," said Leon. "We will start out slowly. It goes like this, slow, slow, sidestep, slow, slow, sidestep." Esther's feet tangled and she caught herself. "You're fine, I've got you," Leon assured. "Keep saying slow, slow, sidestep until you get the hang of it. We won't try any fancy steps, yet." They made it all the way around the dance floor, once, with Esther watching her feet and repeating the words.

"We made it," said Esther and immediately tangled her feet.

Leon chuckled, "Only the advanced dancers can do the Foxtrot and talk at the same time." Esther went back to watching her feet and repeating the mantra. At last the band played the final notes and Leon finished off with a twirl and a slow dip. "You did well for the first time," complimented Leon, "Shall we look over the refreshment table?"

"I could use a something to drink."

"I'll fetch us two lemonades," said Leon as he turned to leave. "Can you wait right here?"

"I'll sit in one of these chairs and watch the dancers for a while."

Leon returned with the drinks and set them on a tiny serving table. "Here you are, a tart drink for a sweet lady." He groaned, "Now I am hopelessly corny. A perfect description, wouldn't you say?"

"Not at all. You are the most handsome, sophisticated gentleman in the room, perhaps in the whole county."

Leon bowed slightly. "Why thank you, Your Highness. I shall treasure your compliment with pride, forever."

She laughed and picked up her lemonade. "Leon, I'd like to stroll out on the deck. Would you agree?"

140

"Yes, my lady, I would like it very much. And perhaps you might favor me with a kiss from time to time."

"You will have to steal it, sir!"

"Come with me, my innocent" said Leon as he lifted his drink, waggled his eyebrows and gave his imaginary handlebar mustache a twist.

High in the sky an occasional fluffy cloud drifted over the full moon to cast a brief shadow on the deck. Leon took advantage of each opportunity to steal a kiss. A few other couples lingered along the far ends of the deck. Leon and Esther leaned against the rail, sipped their drinks and watched a pair of swans drift by and disappear around the corner.

"I wonder if the duck family has bedded down for the night," she mused.

"I suppose they have located a safe patch of deep grass by now. Are you having fun, ducky?" he asked.

"Oh Leon, this is best time of my life."

Leon leaned down and kissed her bare neck and shoulders. "Mm, me too. Are you finished with your lemonade?"

"Yes, I've had quite enough," she answered.

"Let me take your glass. I hear them playing another Foxtrot. I shall teach you another new dance. Some call this a two-step or just another variation on the Foxtrot. Are you ready for this?"

"I'm game," said Esther.

Leon set the empty glasses on a passing waiter's tray. "Now, the steps will always be the same, slow, slow, quickstep, but this time we will both face the direction of dance, side by side and we won't do any side step. We will just dance in a forward direction. We can either lock our arms together like this, or we can simply hold hands, like this."

He took her left hand in his right and started off. They advanced all the way around the outer edges of the dance floor with no more than one or two glitches. Esther began to feel rather confident. "This isn't so hard," she said and immediately missed a step but quickly changed feet to match with his.

"I warned you about talking," Leon chuckled as he expertly swung around in front of her and continue to lead while he danced backwards. "See how easy it is to switch positions," he said. "We will practice switching a few times. You just need to follow the man. My job is to hold you firmly, like this, so you can feel by my hands and body when it is time to turn." He effortlessly danced and talked at the same time. "The next thing I will teach you is how *you* can dance backwards to my forwards."

"Oh, I don't think so," said Esther as she watched her feet.

Just then Leon swung her around and before she knew it she was dancing backwards. "See how easy it is?"

Esther merely watched her feet and repeated, "Slow, slow, quickstep."

Leon chuckled and resisted doing a fancy twirl. The band paused momentarily and then swung into a fast dance giving the rhythm section, consisting of string bass, guitar, banjo and drums, a chance to demonstrate its skill. More than half the dance couples took to the sidelines, filled up the chairs and crowded the refreshment tables. Leon led Esther to a viewing area. "Let's take a break and watch the fast dancers do their thing," he suggested. Esther was more than willing.

They watched with interest as several trendy dancing couples commanded the center floor while a few diehards continued to slow dance in resistance to the strong jazz beat. Now and then one couple would cut loose with an innovative and flashy exhibition to applause from the sidelines. "There are several new versions of the fast dance coming from the East Coast," remarked Leon. "It's all the rage."

"Along with bootleg liquor, I hear," added Esther.

"Now where did your sheltered tender ears hear of such a scandalous thing?" asked Leon.

142

"It's just something Bill discussed at supper the other night. I think he ordered some for the wedding."

"Aha, I see," said Leon. "Then I guess it's all right."

"Oh you kid!" Esther grinned and gave his arm a tap.

"Now, I am really worried," said Leon.

"Don't worry," laughed Esther. "I actually heard one of the church ladies say it."

"Shocking!" mocked Leon, "Some church lady!"

"Truth," Esther giggled.

"Let's not push this 'truth' thing too far," he retorted.

"One can never push truth too far, can one?" she asked innocently.

"Humph, I do believe you've got me, there," he submitted.

The band struck up a waltz. Leon stood and held out his hand. "At last, a waltz meant for us." She melted into his arms. He twirled her twice around with joyous abandon. Esther's eyes were all for him. Leon pressed his cheek to the top of her head and drew her close. She was aware of the firm length of his body and his muscled thighs as they brushed against hers. "As long as there are young lovers, this dance will never go out of style," he said as he twirled her around a corner.

Esther forgot about her feet and enjoyed floating in his arms. They danced as though they were meant for each other. Leon hummed softly in her ear as he skillfully guided her past a knot of dancers. Esther inhaled his faint masculine scent, a combination of soap, clean clothes, skin and warmth. Her heart was at peace for the first time in months.

***

On the way toward Esther's home, Leon's arms encircled her as she leaned back against his broad chest and sighed. No words were needed as she relaxed to the rhythmic clip-clop of the horses and the regular squeak of the carriage wheels. Her eyelids became heavy.

143

"We are here, Cinderella, just before the midnight chime of the cathedral bells." Leon helped her to alight and walked her to her door.

"Thank you for a magical evening, Leon."

"It was my pleasure, indeed," he whispered as he took her into his arms and gave her a lingering kiss. "I would like to see you at least once during the week and take you to a new place next Saturday night."

"Whatever you want to do, I know I will love it. Don't forget we have Doris and Bill's wedding the following weekend."

"Next Saturday, please dress for dinner and a night on the town. We will be indoors most of the time; but we won't be dancing. Shall we say six-thirty?"

"Six-thirty Saturday night is fine."

"Excellent. And I won't forget the wedding, either"

She gave him a quick kiss and disappeared inside.

***

Saturday night, Leon picked her up in the buggy. They dined at the same restaurant in town where he had taken her on their very first date. Leon checked his pocket watch, one of the few mementos he owned of his father's. "Are you about finished?" asked Leon. "We need to be leaving soon."

"Just let me freshen up and then I'll be ready."

"I'll bring the rig around and meet you out front," said Leon.

They headed back up the street the way they came. Esther wondered where they were going, but she went along with Leon's surprise. Back uptown, he guided his team into one of the hitching posts in front of the opera house. The marquee advertised a motion picture and vaudeville show starring some of the current favorites.

Esther and Leon settled themselves into balcony seats with drinks and a huge bag of popcorn. "We will see Mary Pickford in her first feature film since her storybook wedding to Douglas Fairbanks, Sr. in March, 1920."

144

"Oh how romantic," sighed Esther. "They are the most handsome couple! Did you hear he had built her a twenty-two-room mansion in Beverly Hills as a wedding gift?"

"Did you know they had to divorce their spouses in order to marry each other and they were lovers for three years before the wedding?"

"Scandalous!"

Images started to flicker and dance on the screen. The velvet curtains opened and a few advertisements flashed on and off before "The Movietone News" began. A picture of the new president, Warren G. Harding came on the screen with his wife Florence beside him. They road in an open touring car, as they smiled and waved at the crowd. Another clip showed Henry Ford dressed in a gray suit with white spats and a top hat. He smiled into the camera and proudly showed off a steady stream of Model T motor cars rolling off his assembly line in Highland Park, Michigan.

Leon whispered in Esther's ear, "How would you like to ride in one of those motor cars, Esther?"

"Oh I'd absolutely love it!" she nodded and leaned her head on his shoulder.

"I have a hankering to own one someday," said Leon.

"Shh!" admonished voices from behind.

They suppressed giggles as they turned their heads back toward the screen. The final report concerned Babe Ruth, "the Bambino," as he hit his fiftieth home run of the year for the New York Yankee's baseball team.

Next up was a vaudeville act, the singing Brox sisters, Bobbe, Dagmar and Lorayne. They were shown touring the country trying out the songs from their forthcoming Broadway musical, Irving Berlin's Music Box Revue. They sang the new song, "Everybody Step" to thunderous applause.

Finally, the main feature film came on starring "America's Sweetheart," Mary Pickford, in "Little Lord Fauntleroy" produced by her new company, United Artists' Studios. Mary played a dual role of the lead character as well as the mother.

By now, both the popcorn and the drinks were consumed. Esther rested her head on Leon's shoulder. "Are you getting a bit sleepy, Little One," asked Leon?

"Perhaps a little," admitted Esther.

"Do you want to head out or stay for the last two acts?" he inquired.

"Do you know what is on?"

"I think it is a tap dancing team followed by a juggling act."

"Well, okay, if you want to stay."

"Your choice," insisted Leon.

"Let's compromise. We will stay for one more act," offered Esther.

"Agreed, tap dancers, only." He offered his hand. "Shake?"

As it turned out the tap dancers were energetic and entertaining and the music was loud and lively. Thus revived, Esther sat up, yawned and came awake. When the act left the stage to a standing ovation, Esther and Leon rose by mutual agreement and made their way to the outer lobby. "Why don't you stand inside while I go get the horse and buggy?" suggested Leon. "If you stand here you can watch for me out the window."

***

Esther scooted over beside Leon. He covered their laps with a blanket and clicked his horse into a slow walk home. The horse knew the way allowing Leon to focus his attention on Esther's lips, neck, shoulders and breasts. He nuzzled her neck and whispered sweet nothings in her ears.

Esther became aware of his hand resting on her breast and then on her hip and places in between. Her body seemed to have a mind of its own. It was all she could do not to squirm closer. She parted her lips and Leon's tongue slipped inside her mouth and tickled her lips. She explored his chest and hard flat stomach with her hand.

146

As she dipped lower, Leon groaned and shifted out of her way. "Not there darling or I will go crazy with wanting you. Maybe someday when you are ready but let me touch you instead." He gently placed his hand over her dress between her legs. "Is this all right with you? I won't frighten you, will I?" She hitched herself a little closer and reached up to kiss him.

He laid her back against the cushions and kissed her with his lips and tongue as their breathing quickened and their hearts raced. Leon opened one eye just in time to tug on the right-hand rein and steer the horse into Esther's driveway. He pulled her up beside him and held the reins with one hand.

They came to a halt at her door. "Let me come around and help you down, darling," he said. He walked her slowly to her door. She leaned on him and found it a little difficult to walk. Leon kissed her thoroughly once more and tore himself away. "Shall I stop by and pick you up for church tomorrow?"

"Yes, please do."

"Is about nine-thirty all right?"

Esther nodded, "How about if I pack a picnic lunch for after church?"

"Great idea! I'll bring the blankets," Leon enthused.

"If it is warm enough, would you like to go swimming?"

"Sure, I will toss in my swim suit, in case."

"Good night, darling."

"Good night, dearest. See you tomorrow."

"Tomorrow won't come soon enough for me."

Esther lay in bed thinking about the evening. She remembered the feeling of Leon's lips on hers, his arms around her, his hands on her breasts, as she drifted off to sleep.

Leon whistled a tuneless melody as he unhitched his horse and led him away into the stables. He watered and fed him a scoop of grain, made sure there was hay in the bin and fresh straw in his stall. While

Gibraltar was busy feeding and drinking Leon curried him down and checked his feet for pebbles. Satisfied all was well, Leon walked to the house and prepared for bed.

He was pleased with the progress of his courtship with Esther. *So far, so good,* he thought. There was still a mountain of reluctance to overcome in his pursuit of his wife in bed. The rape left her completely shattered and so uptight she was unable to relax and enjoy a normal sexual experience. In fact, she was so innocent; he doubted she had any idea what she was missing. *Well, it's up to me to teach her, a little bit at a time.*

***

Esther wore a jacket and matching sundress with tiny straps and a full skirt cinched in at the waist with a bright red belt. A matching red ribbon was bowed saucily on the side of her picture straw hat. Leon's eyes bugged out when he saw her. "You look so beautiful this morning darling, but isn't your outfit a little too nice for a picnic?" He relieved her of the lunch basket and placed it in the storage trunk of the buggy.

She tossed in a pair of sandals for later along with her swimsuit and some towels. "Wait until you see how I convert it to a picnic outfit after church," she said. "You look handsome yourself. Did you have a good sleep and pleasant dreams?"

Leon helped her into the buggy and jumped in beside her. "Yes, I did, thank you, and my dreams were all of you," he click-clicked at the horse to start towards their church.

"Oh come now, you flatterer, tell me, what did you *really* dream about?"

"Truth?" He grinned at her and gave the reins a little flip.

"Now you've got my curiosity up… all right, truth."

"Well, I dreamed we were together in our new home," he began while putting one arm around her, "And I was carrying you up to our bedroom." He leaned over and gave her a lingering kiss on the mouth, "And I was unbuttoning your dress." He ran his hand along her cheek

148

and down her arm, "I was removing your clothes and laying you back on the bed." He stroked her leg and whispered in her ear, "And then I removed my clothes and lay down next to you." He slid his hand inside her dress, "Then I put my arms around you and pulled you close." He took her chin in his hand and turned her face toward him, put both arms around her and kissed her thoroughly before he turned back to his driving.

Esther's whole body felt hot and tingly. Her mouth was swollen from his kisses, her cheeks burned and she felt an uncomfortable ache between her legs and in her breasts.

They rode in silence for a while, Leon hummed softly to himself, Esther gazed distractedly at her hands in her lap.

Finally she found her voice, "Was there more? I mean did it just end there?" she murmured, without looking up.

He tipped up her chin with one finger. "What do you mean, did it just end there?" Leon asked with a wicked grin.

"I mean what happened next? Wasn't there more to the dream?"

Leon turned her face to him, "My darling Esther, *you* must complete the dream. When you are ready, you will finish the dream."

***

After church as they were on their way to the lake, Esther folded her jacket, rolled down her stockings, removed her shoes and donned her sandals. She removed the pins from her hair, loosened it into a lush silken cascade and gave her head a toss, "I'm ready for a picnic Leon, what do you think?"

Leon took in her outfit, the red belt, her tiny waist, the matching red bow on the picture hat, the bare shoulders and the glorious hair. He declared, "You more than pass inspection, my pretty maid. May I hold your hand?"

"Yes, please do and hurry." She laughed.

***

Leon leaped down from the buggy, removed his suit coat and tie and laid them across the seat, rolled up his sleeves and grabbed a couple of blankets. Next thing he knew he was hurrying to keep up. First they explored the lakeshore. Esther felt of the water. "Ooo, a bit too cool for my taste"

Leon expertly skipped a stone across the surface.

"Let me try," said Esther eagerly as she picked up a nice large stone and tossed it underhanded into the lake. Ker-plunk! It sank straight down into the depths. She looked at Leon and laughed. "All right, I surrender. Show me how this is done."

"With pleasure, my pretty." He bent and selected a handful of small flat stones. "Like this," he demonstrated. "Fling it sidearm. You want the flat side to hit the water a glancing blow." Leon's stone skipped. "One-two-three-four-five. Not a bad record." He polished his nails with feigned modesty.

Leon handed her a stone and placed his arms around her. "Turn your body sideways, okay." He placed her hand in his. "Grasp the stone flat side down. Hold it between your thumb and forefinger. Now, keep the flat side down. Okay, now we are going to bend over slightly and pull your arm back." Leon spread his legs and fitted her nice bottom into his groin, making sure his arm brushed against her breasts.

She wiggled, "Leon, will you stop it?"

"Whatever do you mean, darling?"

"I think you know perfectly well what I mean. How am I supposed to concentrate on what I'm doing when you are distracting me?"

"Oh, am I being distracting?"

"Yes, you are!"

"Good!" Leon chuckled.

Esther gave his hand a little swat and pretended to pull away. "Now, like this?" She let go with a mighty overhand throw. Ker-plunk! Her stone made a splash and sank.

"Not so much overhand, Little One. Try a sidearm throw." He took her arm and guided it into a perfect pitch.

In unison they counted, "One-two-three!"

"I did it! I did it!" Esther jumped up and down, threw her arms around Leon and continued jumping up and down. "Yeah for me!"

Leon held her close and stood still. "Do that some more," he grinned at her.

She stood still and blushed. She cleared her throat. "Uh, well, uh, I um. Thank you for the demonstration, sir." She turned and walked away, hiding her smile.

Leon hurried to catch up with her, took her hand and swung it as they strolled off toward the trees. "Let's explore those pine trees over there," he pointed. A small clearing opened almost completely hidden from the lake. The sun shone in the center of a grassy area. "Listen," he said, "Do you hear anything?" A faint breeze whispered through the pine needles and brought a fresh scent to their nostrils.

"It's really quiet and peaceful here, isn't it?" Esther inhaled deeply, "Smells good, too."

"Shall I spread our blankets here?" asked Leon.

"Perfect. Let's do it." She helped him spread the blanket out on the grass in a shady area.

"Will you please make yourself at home while I run down and fetch the picnic basket?"

"This is enchanting," she said as she settled gracefully on the blanket.

Leon tossed the second folded blanket onto her lap and headed off. In no time he returned with the basket, set it to one side and settled down next to her, leaning back on his elbows. He gazed up at the clear blue sky and a few fluffy white clouds. He smiled over at her, patted the blanket next to him and invited, "Care to join me?"

Esther rolled the spare blanket into a pillow and put it under his head. Then she laid her head on his chest and breathed a sigh. Leon put his arm around her body. "Heaven," he said.

"I enjoyed sitting beside you at church," she said. "You looked so handsome, wise and intelligent, I felt proud."

"I had trouble concentrating on the message, today," Leon confessed. "Was too distracted thinking about you sitting there, hiding under your enormous hat," he observed.

"Oh, was there a message? I think I missed it," she giggled.

"Well now, young lady, you should have paid attention, because here is the quiz: Name three Biblical incidents the preacher used in the sermon today."

"Noah and the Ark?"

"Wrong…strike one."

"Abraham?"

"Be specific."

"The archangel visits Abraham?"

"Strike two."

"Um…I'd better get this one right. Solomon builds the temple?"

"You're out! Pay up"

"What's this pay up nonsense? I never agreed to a bet."

"I seem to remember you did."

"Well, first tell me: what's the penalty?"

"The loser has to forfeit one kiss."

"Oh well, easy." She bent quickly and gave him a kiss on the cheek."

"Hey, wait a minute. Come on, pay up."

"You said 'one kiss,' didn't you?"

"A peck on the cheek does not a kiss make. Come here and give me a real kiss," he puckered up.

As Esther leaned over his face her hair fell in a screen around them. Brown eyes locked onto blue. She framed his face with her hands and came closer with excruciating slowness. Leon held his breath. She touched noses and pulled back a few inches, keeping her eyes on his without blinking. She brushed her lips on his. Her tongue licked his lips in feather touches.

Oh God! Leon held perfectly still. Sparks seemed to fly when their lips touched. He felt an uncomfortable tightness growing in his loins. *Oh God in Heaven, please make this the beginning for Esther. Show me how to please her. Guide my body, hands and lips. Make me aware of her every need.*

Her eyelids slowly lowered, half way closed, as she tilted her head to the right and affixed her soft lips to his. She settled her breasts against his chest, put her arms around him and pulled him over on his side. Leon turned slightly toward her, adjusted his arms around her, fitted their bodies together and deepened the kiss. She moved to place one leg over his. They remained in this position and kissed and kissed. He whispered to her, "Esther, my darling," between kisses. "Esther, darling, can you feel how much I want you?"

Her answer was to snuggle her groin area against his hardness, move against him and moan. He restrained himself as she moved to get closer. He carefully placed one hand on her breast. She nuzzled his neck and raked it with her teeth, he moved his head to allow her better access. She reached up and pulled her straps down on one side baring her soft breast to his big hand. "May I kiss you there?" he asked. She responded by moving her breast toward his lips. Leon fitted his mouth to her breast and suckled as Esther arched her body and moaned.

He moved his hand back to cover the breast and she adjusted. Leon pressed in a little harder and Esther moved against him. He began to rub gently and she moaned in satisfaction. As he carefully commenced to massage her, she fairly hummed. He planted kisses on her face, her neck, her breast, her lips, as he continued his efforts.

A soft breeze cooled his sweat. Nothing was heard save their breathing in unison and an occasional bird's chirp in the trees. They felt alone, a million miles from anywhere. "Darling," he whispered. "This is all right, because we are married. Just enjoy. This is wonderful for me, too. But we will proceed only so far as you want. I promise I will stop anytime you say so." *Not sure I can keep such a promise without Your help, Lord.*

She answered by drawing his mouth to hers, tugging his shirt out of his pants and putting her hand on his bare chest. "All right," he panted, "You are safe with me." He pulled the extra blanket over them for a bit of privacy, settled her mouth against his, and wrapped her body around his. Esther opened her legs to his clever, searching fingers. For several minutes they were lost in each other, as Esther relaxed and let herself respond with increased intensity until she ground into his hand, cried out and reached for complete fulfillment.

Gradually Esther began to come down off her high, opening her eyes and began showering his head and face with kisses. She collapsed in wonderment against his chest, limp and satiated. She closed her eyes inhaled deeply, sighed and threw the covering blanket back. Leon smoothed down her dress and adjusted her bodice. He smiled at her, slowly stroked her body and kissed her forehead from time to time. His heart was bursting. There were no words to describe his sense of relief. *Thank you, thank you God. She's my wife now. What a marvelous day!*

***

CHAPTER TWENTY-FOUR – At the Grave

The weeks of summer flew by. Doris and Bill's wedding was beautiful and fun for Esther. She served as matron of honor and couldn't help but remember her own wedding and the vows she made. She thought of the good times and bad she and Leon had been through and how Leon had been faithful to his vows.

In the weeks before Doris's wedding, Esther had sensed a cooling of her relationship with her sister. She suspected Bill disapproved of Esther's pregnancy and the timing of Baby Girl's conception which had become apparent with the birth of Baby. Clearly it happened before marriage. Doris would never say anything to Esther, but Bill may have planted doubts in her head. Perhaps she was even feeling shamed by it all. It would be lonely without Doris, but maybe it was just as well.

Leon's attentions to her since they made their bargain had been a godsend, thus Esther's hopes were gradually returning.

***

During the weeks following Baby's death, Leon became increasingly puzzled by the strange bouquets of wildflowers he found when he visited the grave. Neither of Esther's family members seemed to have left them. One evening Leon brought it up at suppertime. None had any idea who else might be visiting the site.

Esther, most of all, vehemently denied it, "Don't ask me to ever visit the grave Leon! I can't do it!"

"But, Esther, surely someday you will want to..."

"No, Leon I refuse to think about it! I'm sorry I just can't!"

Millie looked at Esther and sadly bit her lip. Later after Esther had excused herself and gone up to her room, Millie looked from Walter to Leon, "I'm afraid Esther has never really dealt with the trauma of the rape. Somehow, I think she is connecting her feelings about the rape to her feelings toward the baby. This may be affecting her attitude toward motherhood. I hope not, but emotions are powerful things."

Walter considered her remarks. "Yes, it can also poison her relationships with the men in her life." Walter seemed to direct his comment at Leon.

"I'll admit it has been a challenge," said Leon, "but I don't blame you or your daughter, not at all."

"I wish there was some way we could help," Millie offered.

"I don't know," said Leon. "If only there was some way she could talk about the rape, get it out, you know? But you heard the way she reacted when I brought it up," he sighed and fiddled with his fork and spoon. "Do you think they will ever catch the rapist? I think it might help. Remember how she was afraid to reveal his name?"

"You never can tell, maybe he'll trip himself up, someday." Walter wished he was free to say more. He vowed he would speak to the mayor and sheriff again next time they were together.

***

Walter entered the township meeting room, hung up his jacket and hat and pulled out a chair. "Evening, Mayor, what's on the agenda of importance?"

"Evening, Walt. Not a whole lot. We should be done early. How is everything out on the farm?"

"Growing, growing," said Walter. "Those little shoots are fairly leaping out of the ground. Say, Dean, if we have time, later, I'd like to have a word with you."

"Sure thing, Walt. Just keep all your remarks short and don't give me a hard time," he chuckled.

"Who me?" Walter feigned innocence. "Now why would I do such thing?"

Dean merely smiled and turned to greet some more arrivals.

The meeting ended early. After the others had left, Dean began loading his notes and papers into a case. "Have a hankering to drop by the house and throw back a few?" he inquired of Walter.

"Thank you kindly, but maybe some other time," answered Walter. "I just wanted to speak to you in private about the situation you mentioned some months ago. It had to do with hiring a detective from the county to come out and work on the serial rape case. I've been curious to know whether you found the guy."

"Oh, yes, I remember the case. Sit down, sit down, Walt. Take a load off your feet."

"Sure, Dean." Walter sat. "Now, about the rape case."

"Seems I remember there were three girls, or was it two, who reported something similar. I think Herb finally had to close the file."

"What do you mean close the file? Good Lord, man, I have two daughters! You can't let Herb just close the file!"

"Now, simmer down, Walt. There simply wasn't any more evidence. You've gotta have evidence to arrest somebody. There are plenty of young bucks around here get kind of wild on a Saturday night, but you can't arrest somebody's son if they haven't committed any crime. There was no way to prove those girls were telling the truth. It was just their say so."

"Oh, for crying out loud! This is so disgusting! You need evidence? Get some evidence, man." Walter jammed his hat on his head, grabbed his jacket and stalked out.

***

Walter was so frustrated he could barely stand it as he drove home in a growing black mood. It was the same old story. Man takes advantage. Strong man forces weaker woman. Woman objects. Big strong man gives her what she "wants" and what she "asked" for. She cries "rape." He cries, "No way, she asked for it." A government run by men, for men, gives the same weight to his word as to hers, maybe more. *If I ever find him, I'm not waiting for any weakling sheriff to come after him. I know what I have to do.*

***

Leon dismounted from Gibraltar and looped his reins around a fence rail. "I'll leave you here for just a few minutes, old friend," he said as he stroked his horse's nose. "I need to run up the hill and see Baby Girl's grave for just a minute, okay? I'll hurry back." Leon was having a busy day. He hurried on up the hill, somewhat distractedly thinking about all he had to do today.

Looking out the kitchen window, Esther noticed Leon's horse tied up at the corral. She turned and walked over to the opposite side of the room and peered out the window. She saw Leon's back disappearing into the woods. *He's going up to the grave. He'll probably stop in when he comes back.* She headed up to her room to freshen up.

Her pulse quickened in anticipation. She could hardly wait to see him again. She hadn't been sleeping well lately, what with tossing and turning, thinking about their date last Sunday. Sometimes she lost track of her tasks, daydreaming about Leon. *Oh my, I'm worse than a teenager. I've got to get a grip on myself!* Her cheeks reddened just thinking about it.

Leon hurried on up the hill. Just then a rabbit darted across his path. Leon hesitated for a minute, chuckling, as he watched the rabbit disappear under a bush. *I'll bet she's got a nest under there with a half dozen little bunny-rabbits. She heard me coming and rushed to protect them.* Leon trudged on at a slightly slower pace.

A large bird swooped down over his head. Leon turned to look. *Must be an owl or some kind of hawk. Maybe a bit upset because I alerted her prey. Better luck next time, Bird. Whoa, wait a minute. Are you trying to tell me something, Lord? Perhaps I should adopt a bit more reverential attitude in approaching a Holy site.*

Leon cautiously approached the clearing and stopped after he stepped out into the edge. He saw a stooped figure standing by the grave, with his back turned. *What on earth?* Leon stood silently for several minutes, observing. The mannerisms seemed more like a man than a woman. The man clutched something in his hand. Leon took a step back and faded into a shadow where he could observe without being seen.

The man seemed to be doing some kind of ritual. He walked slowly around the grave, keeping his eyes on the ground. Now and then he bent to pick something off the grave, a pebble or a stick, maybe. It was hard to tell. Then he seemed to brush back the existing dead flowers on the grave. He picked some nearby grasses and spread them over the grave and then he placed his tiny bouquet of wildflowers right in the center. He bowed his head and seemed to be mumbling something. He wiped his eyes and straightened.

As the man turned away from the grave, Leon stepped out of the shadows. To the startled little man, Leon appeared ten feet tall with lightning coming out of his eyes. The man halted in fright.

"Otis! What the devil are you doing here?" Leon shouted. He strode forward with powerful determination in every step. "Speak up, man, answer me!" Leon demanded.

"I-I ain't doin' nuthin'," stammered Otis.

Leon stepped up to the grave and examined the weeds and wildflowers. He abruptly turned. "You! You're the one!" he roared. Leon stabbed a finger in Otis's chest and backed him up. "You!"

"I don't mean no trouble. I don't mean no harm," trembled Otis. "Leave m-me alone," he begged as he backed away.

"You've got no right. This is my Baby's grave!" said Leon. "You've been messing up my Baby's grave for weeks!"

"N-no!" screamed Otis. "Not your b-baby! M-my baby!" He slapped his hand on his chest, tears rolling down his face. "M-my baby died. I want m-my b-baby," he wailed amid terrible sobs.

The color drained from Leon's face as he stared at Otis in utter horror. Leon lunged for Otis, grasped him by the lapels and pulled Otis's face into his own. When he spoke, his voice had ice in it. "What are you talking about? What did you do to Esther, Otis? Tell me the truth or I will kill you right here and bury you right now!"

"I-I j-just luv Esther. She's purty." Otis flinched and tried to turn away.

"What did you do to her?" Leon shook him and set him down hard.

"Well, I d-don't know wha' cha calls it. Sumpin,' ya know. Just sumpin.'"

"Did you take this piece hanging between your legs and put it inside of Esther's legs?" Leon took hold of Otis's penis.

Otis nodded his head, yes, and grinned, showing his dirty teeth.

"What about other girls, in town, did you do the same thing to any of them?"

Otis nodded again, "I luv g-girls. Thar real purty."

Leon glared at Otis with utter loathing. He now understood the full weight of what Otis had done to Esther and how incredibly brave Esther had been under the burden. Leon suddenly realized he loved Esther with all his heart, with his very life. This worm, this creep, had done something so horrible to her even Leon couldn't speak of it. *Oh God.*

"You are lower than a worm, you dirty little man. Now, listen to me and you listen **well**. You have no right to this baby. You are not to come up here again, ever!" Otis quivered in sheer terror. "Esther is my wife, do you hear me? You are to stay away from her and all other girls. Do you understand?" Leon demanded.

"No," Otis shook his head. "Why?"

"Because Esther did not want you touching her. Do not touch any woman unless she wants you. It's wrong. Very wrong." Leon looked around and glanced toward heaven. "*Lord...Lord...*" was his anguished cry. He stood still, just staring at Otis who whimpered and cowered out of reach now. Leon's powerful chest heaved. "You dirty, pitiful little man." Leon shook his head sadly and spat. "I'm loath to touch you, but come here," he commanded.

Otis cringed and wiped his nose on his sleeve.

Leon took hold of the back of Otis's jacket and pulled him up. "Come on, I'm taking you back to the barn." Leon marched him down the hill. Otis lurched and stumbled over nothing in particular. Leon just set him on his feet and kept moving with purpose in every step.

They arrived in the barnyard, into the horse barn, past the stalls and banged on Walter's office door. "Go on in, the door's open," said Walter, coming up behind them.

Leon gave Otis a shove and propelled him into the office. "Here's your man," Leon said. "Here's your rapist!" He spat. "Lock him up and send for the sheriff."

"Oh, dear God!" Walter exclaimed. "Otis, God in Heaven, how could you do such a thing?"

"I-I d-didn't hurt nobody," sniveled Otis.

"Tell Walter what you did to Esther and to those girls in town, Otis," instructed Leon.

"I j-just took my thingee, ya know, this here thingee between my legs and I put it between thar l-legs. That's all I did, yesirree. I kept shoving it as far as it would g-go," he tittered.

"Oh, but Otis, I think you hit Esther, too."

"Yes, c-cuz she wouldn't hold still 'n' she wouldn't shut up. I had ta shut her up so I could do it, ya know."

The saddest look came over Walter's face and tears formed in his eyes. He looked up at Leon, slowly shook his head and looked down again.

"Lock him up, Walter. I'll go for the sheriff."

Walter heaved a big sigh and cleared his throat. "Come along, Otis."

Leon grabbed the reins on Gibraltar, leaped into the saddle and headed toward town.

Esther turned from the window, a puzzled look on her face. She said something to Millie and then turned back to her work.

***

CHAPTER TWENTY-FIVE – Family Circle

So long as the rapist had remained anonymous, Walter's feelings toward him had been white-hot, but now since Otis' guilt had been uncovered, Walter's rage seemed to fade and turn to a confused amalgam of anger, pity, pain, sorrow and empathy.

"Come along with me, Otis," said Walter. "I need to make sure you can't run away before the sheriff gets here." Walter led Otis into one of the secure storage rooms. He grabbed some stout rope and a straight-backed chair, dragging it into the room. "Sit here, Otis" he directed. "Now put your hands behind your back please." Walter made sure Otis was securely tied without hurting the man.

"W-what are ya doin' Mr. Boss-man?" Otis whined.

Walter placed a hand on Otis's shoulder. "You have to stay here and wait until the sheriff comes to take you away. It won't be too long. If it takes longer than an hour, I will bring you some food and something to drink."

Otis began quietly crying, his eyes following Walter as he turned to leave the room. Walter paused and turned back to gaze at the pitiful sight. "You have been a help to me, Otis. Everything will be all right."

Walter sighed, left the room, closed the door and snapped the padlock. He headed for the house and entered the kitchen.

"Hi, honey," said Millie as she reached for two cups and began filling them with coffee.

"Add another cup to the order please," said Walter, "I need to talk to you and Esther both. Also, I'll need to talk to Doris and Bill, too, next time they stop over."

"This sounds serious," said Millie. "I'll call Esther." Millie went to the stairwell and called Esther down from her room.

162

"Hello, Father," said Esther.

"Please have a seat, Esther," said Walter. "Something important has happened I need to tell you about."

Two pairs of eyes were on Walter. "What is it?" asked Millie.

"Millie. Esther. I have some news." Walter drew a deep breath and blew it out, "Esther, it seems your rapist has been found." Esther gasped. Her hand flew to her mouth, her eyes popped. "You don't need to hold it in, anymore, honey. Otis has confessed."

"Oh my Lord!" exclaimed Millie. "Are you certain it was Otis? Of course, you're certain. What happened?"

"Leon discovered Otis at the grave site messing around and putting weeds on the grave. Leon put two and two together and confronted Otis. Otis confessed to the whole thing. Then Leon brought Otis to me, and Otis told it over again in my presence. I believe it's true. Otis committed at least four rapes we know of. There may have been more."

"But why? How could he do such a thing?" asked Millie.

"Well, it seems he was just following his instincts. We misjudged him. Although he is just a simple, loveable, uneducated man, we should have realized Otis doesn't know right from wrong. He likes girls and was doing what comes naturally. In a way we have ourselves to blame for allowing him the freedom, but I don't know how we could have stopped him."

"Oh my goodness, Walter, I practically forced Esther to ride into town with Otis. She all but refused to ride with him but I insisted. What have I done to my own daughter?" Millie cried.

Esther's stomach clutched up. "You didn't know, Mother."

"It didn't occur to me to wonder why you refused to ever ride with him again," said Millie. "I simply accepted your explanation his smell made you nauseous."

Millie's eyes met Esther's, "How can you ever forgive me?"

"There's nothing to forgive, Mother," said Esther. "I sensed at the time I shouldn't go with Otis. It must have been my guardian angel warning me. I should have refused. It is as much my fault as anyone's."

"You've held it in all this time, you poor darling," Millie wailed.

"I had to remain silent because Father threatened to kill the rapist. I couldn't allow my own father to become a murderer."

"You were right, Esther," said Walter. "I said it and I meant it, too; but when the time came I couldn't harm him. He had no idea what he did was wrong. Otis is locked up in the barn."

"What will happen to him?" asked Esther.

"Leon has gone into town for the sheriff. They will take him away, I'm sure. Then it is up to the justice system to handle, swiftly I hope."

"He'll be taken to the jail?" asked Esther.

"Within the hour. You have nothing more to fear, my darling daughter."

Esther's eyes were brimming.

Walter rose from his chair and held out his arms. "Come here, my darlings." Both Esther and Millie moved into his strong embrace. Esther sniffed and sobbed. Walter held them until Esther quieted. "You are going to heal, now, Esther," he said. "You can thank your loving husband for catching this guy. It's time you told Leon the whole story and put it behind you." Fresh sobs ensued, but it was hard to tell who cried and who comforted.

At last they parted and sat back down to three cold cups of coffee.

***

PART FOUR

CHAPTER TWENTY-SIX – The Tin Lizzie

Esther struggled down the stairs with the last of her suitcases, just as she heard a peculiar horn sounding from the direction of the driveway. She hurried to the door and came face to face with a broad chest blocking her view.

Leon's impish grin seemed to light up her world. "Close those beautiful brown eyes," he invited.

Esther backed away from the door, closed her eyes and held out her hand. Leon took her hand and guided her carefully outside. "Okay, you can open your eyes, now. Surprise!"

"Oh my goodness, where did you get the Model T? It's beautiful!"

"A beautiful automobile for a beautiful lady. It's yours, Esther, but only if you will let me drive occasionally," Leon added with a twinkle.

"What a surprise! I never dreamed! But, how did you get this? You didn't use your savings, I hope," accused Esther, being practical. After all, she was planning for Leon to use his money to buy them their first home, with plenty of bedrooms for their large family she planned to have as soon as possible.

"Let's just say I made a very favorable trade. I relieved a frustrated elderly gentleman of his newfangled horseless carriage in exchange for the fastest riding horse in the county."

"Not Gibraltar?"

"This is progress, Esther. And, besides, I relieved him of a rather nice piece of change in the process. From now on, no more dirty stalls to clean out, no more buggies. This is your new chariot. Don't I look rather debonair standing here? Do you want to take my picture?"

"Oh, go on you!" Esther gave his arm a friendly tap.

"Come, let me help you in. I'll load your suitcases in the back and we'll be off on our honeymoon. This time it will be a real honeymoon. I guarantee it."

Millie and Walter came out on the steps to watch the young couple off and wave them goodbye. Leon came back and kissed Millie on the cheek, "Goodbye, Mother, for a few days." He took Walter's hand. "I can't thank you enough for everything."

"You two have a wonderful time. God bless," said Walter.

Leon reached in on the driver's side and double checked that the brake was set and the gear shift in neutral. He grabbed a special crank out of the back and proceeded to fit it into a drive-shaft in the front of the engine. Leon rolled up his sleeves and started turning the crank. On the third try the engine caught, then sputtered and died. Leon laughed, "It takes a few tries for this to work. Push in on the knob marked choke, please, Esther."

This time he gave it four full turns. The engine caught and sputtered to life. A happy new sound filled the air: ka-chug, ka-chug, ka-chug, ka-chug. Leon ran for the driver's seat, mounted up, slammed the door shut and stomped in the clutch. "We'll let the engine warm up for just a minute," he grinned at Esther.

He turned to the front, released the brake, shifted into low, gave it a little gas and let out the clutch. The motorcar lurched forward. "Sorry, it's a bit jerky. I haven't quite got the hang of it," offered Leon by way of apology. "Wave goodbye, Esther."

Esther recovered her balance and looked around for something to hang onto. She turned back and gaily waved to her parents who were watching them leave. Millie and Walter each lifted an arm.

"We're off," exulted Leon, "Niagara Falls, here we come!"

"I hope you aren't planning to drive this thing all the way to Ontario," shouted Esther over the noise of the engine.

"No, no, only as far as Jackson, where we catch our train at ten o'clock tonight. We will have a sleeping car all the way. Tomorrow morning, after breakfast in the dining car we'll arrive at Niagara. Then we'll catch a taxicab over to our hotel which overlooks the falls."

Esther nodded in relief and grabbed her hat as their speed increased to almost twenty-two miles per hour. The trees seemed to blur by on the right causing a bit of nausea. Esther turned her eyes and watched straight ahead. This seemed to stop the spinning sensation.

Leon happily tooted the horn, "Ooo-ga, Ooo-ga," and again, "Ooo-ga, Ooo-ga," and he laughed.

Esther gazed at her husband's profile. "It is wonderful to see you smiling again," she noted.

"I've got so much to smile about. Let's be happy. Let's enjoy ourselves. We're going to have a great time, aren't we?"

"I agree," said Esther. "I am so relieved and happy I can hardly stand it."

"What a day!" exulted Leon. "The sun is shining, the grass is green and the sky is blue. Here I am driving my brand-new Model T Ford with the love of my life sitting by my side. What more could a fellow want?"

"Did you say, 'the *love* of your life'?"

"Yes Esther, you are the one and only love of my life, for now and forever. I will love you till the end of time." He looked at her and took her hand. Leon threw in the clutch and put his right foot on the brake pedal. The automobile cruised to a stop. Leon put the gear shift in neutral and set the hand-brake. He took Esther in his arms. "I love you, Esther. I love you more than life. I cannot live without you. Darling, will you marry me, all over again?"

"Yes, I'll marry you," she said, her eyes brimming.

"I need to know, something," said Leon. "Can you tell me you love me, too, just a little bit?" *Please God.* He breathed.

"Not a little bit, Leon." For a second his heart sank, but then she continued, "I love you with all my heart."

Leon grinned from ear to ear and drew her close for a long kiss. Both hearts fluttered and did several flips. "You have made me the happiest man alive. I love you so much." *Thank you, God!*

"I love you, too," said Esther.

"What say we make this our really true honeymoon? Is it possible?"

"Yes, darling. I believe I'm ready."

Another kiss and then Leon turned to drive. "You won't regret it," he promised and his heart soared. He smiled as they picked up speed and began to sing, "Let me call you 'Sweetheart', I'm in love with you. Let me hear you whisper that you love me, too." Esther joined in, "Keep the love-light glowing in your eyes so true." They finished in harmony, "Let me call you Sweetheart, I'm in love with you."

***

CHAPTER TWENTY-SEVEN – Niagara Falls, Ontario, Canada

Leon helped his bride down from the Pullman car. Their bags were already loaded onto a luggage cart. "Please show us to the taxi stand. We'll be staying at the Clifton Hotel."

"Yes, sir, Clifton is the very best hotel. Please step over here, sir."

Esther was thrilled to pieces as she watched out the window. "Look, Leon! Oh! Look at the falls! Incredible!" Leon was tickled to watch her reaction. His young bride, born and raised on a farm, had never journeyed more than ten or twenty miles from home and yet she gazed out the window at one of the great wonders of the world.

Meanwhile their driver kept up a running commentary of statistics. "One fifth of the world's fresh water comes from the top four Great Lakes, passing over the falls and down the Niagara River to Lake Ontario; from there it flows down the St. Lawrence River to the Atlantic Ocean. No more than one percent of the water is new. The rest is melted glacier water. Niagara is the second largest falls in the world, second only to Victoria Falls in southern Africa...."

Esther gaped in wonder as both falls came into view.

Leon quoted from a brochure they had picked up on the train. "Listen to Rupert Brooke's description of the Canadian falls, 'The white and blue and slate color of the water blends into a rich, wonderful, luminous green. Then with a slow grandeur, it plunges into eternal thunder and white chaos below.'"

Esther glanced over Leon's shoulder and continued reading, "Both violet and green colored water frays and frills to white as it falls. The mass of water, striking some hidden base of rock, leaps up the whole two hundred feet again in pinnacles and cones of spray."

Their taxi delivered them to the front door of the Clifton Hotel. They were met by two uniformed doormen who swung open the doors with a flourish. A third man handled their luggage. "Welcome to

Clifton Hotel," a smiling assistant manager greeted them, "Right this way Mr. and Mrs. Douglas. Congratulations on your marriage." Clearly, the man thought they were newlyweds.

Indeed, Esther had no desire to disabuse him of the notion. She felt exactly as if she was a new bride and looked forward to their first night in the same bed in six months.

Leon signed the register. A bellhop showed them to the bridal suite on the top floor with a sweeping panorama of windows overlooking the American and Canadian Falls and the Rainbow Bridge.

Their suite was decorated with exquisite French furniture, oriental rugs, double hung gold and white draperies. Esther tested the huge canopied bed, placed her purse on the delicate lady's desk and pushed aside the pen, ink and embossed stationery. She moved into the sitting room and chose a comfortable chair from which she could see the falls.

"May I light the fire for you?" asked the bellman.

"Yes, by all means, but do it later when you deliver our lunch," answered Leon. The bellman showed him the amenities of their rooms while a maid unpacked their suitcases into the matching armoires, and discretely left by a side entrance.

Leon placed a luncheon order with the bellman to be delivered in two hours and gave him a nice tip. The bellman bowed out the door.

Without a word, Leon turned to her and opened his arms. Esther rushed into them. Leon picked her up and twirled her around. They laughed aloud as he set her down carefully. She took both his hands in hers and fairly danced in a circle as she pulled his shirttail out of his pants. Leon was going crazy with laughter. She grabbed his belt, slipped it out of his pants and gave it a toss. She knelt down and pulled the ties on his shoes. Then she started to do a strip tease, remove her own clothes and scatter them around the room. Leon chased her as she giggled and dodged out of his grasp. Off came her dress as she ran behind a chair. He climbed over the chair and reached for her. Once more she slipped away and ran for the bedroom with

170

Leon close on her heels. She stopped suddenly allowing him to run into her. She turned on him and backed him up against the bed. Leon was wild with laughter, his heart bursting with love and praise to God.

Esther reached out one dainty hand, gave him a shove and Leon crashed onto the bed. Esther dove on top of him, wrapped her legs around him and started to tickle. "Ha, I think you are ticklish in this spot here!" she laughed, "and here…and here." Leon was writhing trying to get away from her torture. "No way, you are not escaping. Not until you give in."

"I give in, I give in," he gasped in between hysterics.

"Not good enough," said Esther as she tickled his feet.

"No, no, stop!" cried Leon in mock terror.

"What do you say?" she demanded.

"Uncle, uncle!" he shouted.

She collapsed onto his chest and began kissing him. He rolled them over and took a position on top. "Aha, now!" he growled, "Prepare for payback!"

She whipped him over and took a position sitting on his stomach, propped on her knees, her palms flat on his chest. "Not so fast, Mr. Douglas; I have you in my clutches and I plan to have my wicked way with you."

"Well, why didn't you say so?" Leon laid his arms and legs flat and open. "Have at it, lady, do your worst."

"Oh, darling," she melted against him curled up against his body and hugged his chest, "I am so happy. I love you so much." She reached up and kissed his chin then laid her ear against his heart, beating strong and loud.

Leon's arms came around her, "I love you too with all my heart. I am so lucky and blessed. Thank you God!" He tipped her chin up and kissed her thoroughly. "What say we pull back the covers and snuggle for a while? Would you like to, darling?"

"I thought you'd never ask."

They slipped under the silken sheets, turned toward each other and smiled. They began to kiss and the world quickly faded away. Their skin felt absolutely delicious to touch. Their hands, arms and legs tangled, sought, touched, stroked, rubbed, and felt as if they could not get enough. There were no tormented memories. All was forgotten in a haze of pure bliss. The more they touched, the more sensitized their skins became until they were on fire and lost in each other.

This time, every soft caress by Leon felt as natural as if it required no thought. He tenderly loved and laved her breasts with his tongue and lips. Neither one noticed who moved first, it seemed to come by mutual agreement.

Esther lifted to him. Leon kissed her reverently and held her. They were a perfectly matched pair, made in heaven to fit together.

Everything in Esther's body called, craved, demanded. *Not yet, God* Leon prayed. *I need to hear her say it.*

Finally she managed to gasp, "Please, Leon, I beg you, take me."

Oh, yes, God, Leon breathed. His member kissed her entrance. She grasped it and eagerly guided their bodies together. They paused getting used to the feeling. The sensation was so far beyond heavenly, he held his breath and focused every atom of his body on it. Now he could proceed with his dream.

Esther felt incredible. All her little signals thrilled and spurred him on. Leon restrained himself until he was sure she was ready. *I'm in no hurry. Please let this last forever*, he prayed as his breath and heart rate increased, out of his control. Esther's breathing increased along with his until she was perspiring and panting. Leon fought the tumult as long as he could. It was time. There was no holding back. Esther cried out as both partners were carried over in the tide.

Leon felt satiated and finished. At last Esther slowed down and her voice hummed in satisfaction. He rolled her over onto his stomach and brought her down to his chest. She showered him with kisses and they held each other, until their bodies cooled and they finally settled down.

He lay there for the longest time, just stroked her body and let the joy in his heart flow and overflow. *Dear Lord, I give you thanks for your love, pouring over and around us. Praise God, my wife is mine at last.*

***

PART FIVE

CHAPTER TWENTY-EIGHT – Kansas

The Model T was loaded to the hilt with possessions. Esther and Millie had worked together right up to the moment of departure, as they marked which goods could be packed in trunks for shipment and which absolutely had to go into the auto for the trip to Kansas.

The day of departure had arrived. The four of them made one last round of emotional goodbyes. Esther was leaving home for good, this time. It could be years before they would return. For the tenth time, Millie and Esther promised to write every week and exchanged one last hug. Leon cranked up the engine, jumped aboard, let out the clutch and they were off.

Leon took his bride away from everything she knew, to begin a new adventure in Kansas. They escaped a firestorm of criticism left behind.

    ***

After Otis was arrested, the inevitable scandal had swept the village. The lives of Esther and the other victims became almost unbearable. Speculation spread like wildfire. The gossips had a field day. Esther had suffered the most humiliation of all because she was the only one of the girls who had become pregnant. Esther bravely held up her head, but trips into church were extremely painful. Things were difficult for Millie and Walter as well, but they tried to not let it show.

A few of the church members treated them with sympathy, more simply turned away. The few who remained openly snubbed them. The most vocal were downright hostile and complained to the pastor. "It is a sacrilege to allow a sinful woman into God's house. She is setting a bad example for our daughters. Get rid of her!" They whispered among themselves, "She asked for it, flouncing around, showing her ankles and riding alone with a man. She deserved to have her baby die. God was punishing her." "Poor Leon, she must have bewitched him, too." At first the pastor tried to stem the tide. A few leaders spoke up in defense of Esther but those voices soon faded into silence when they realized their own positions were in jeopardy. The harsher voices prevailed.

Between them, Leon and Esther had decided it would be best for everyone if they left. Leon's employer had connections in Kansas and offered to write an inquiry on Leon's behalf. He wrote a glowing letter of recommendation. A positive job offer came by return mail. The job wouldn't be on a farm, but it would provide a decent living for the two of them. A rental house came with it. Leon would be driving a delivery truck. He loved to drive and Leon would do anything to support his wife. He and Esther talked it over and decided to accept.

***

The flivver was equipped with every possible tool, replacement parts, spare tires, extra cans of gasoline and oil. It would be a trip of more than seven hundred miles through Michigan, Indiana, Illinois and Missouri over some well-maintained roads and some others which were little more than cattle trails. If only the weather would cooperate, they hoped to make as much as one to two hundred miles on a good day. Allowing for the unexpected, it could take upwards of a week or two to make the trip.

The first day on the road went well. It was a relief to get on their way. With one hand on the wheel, Leon leaned over to his bride and planted a kiss. "Feel like talking or singing, he asked?"

"Sure," Esther said, "You go first."

"Do you think it is about time we gave this flivver a name? I'm thinking of something more personal than Flivver or Model T?"

"Wonderful idea," answered Esther. "Let's think of a name. After all she is taking the place of a family member. If we treat her right, maybe she will perform for us."

"How about 'Lizzie?'" Leon asked.

"I'm thinking of something more distinguished," mused Esther, "Besides all the other Model Ts are called Lizzie, short for Tin Lizzie."

"Oh, yes, of course," agreed Leon.

"Perhaps something along the lines of a prize stallion, but more modern," offered Esther.

"More like a mare than a stallion, don't you think?" asked Leon. "Aren't motorcars female?

"If she were a male we could call her Gibraltar."

"What would be the female version of Gibraltar?" Leon posed.

"Gibra?" suggested Esther.

"Gib?"

"Gibby?"

"Yes, let's call her Gibby!"

"Except, we have to change the spelling to J-i-b-b-i-e."

"I like it. Jibbie, it is. Jibbie, the Lizzie!" They both dissolved into laughter. It took very little to make them laugh, these days. "Perhaps you can compose a limerick about Miss Jibbie, the Tin Lizzie," suggested Leon.

"There is no shortage of spare time to work on such things," observed Esther, as they passed through another small town. "I'd rather think about the wonderful time we had in Niagara Falls. You planned the ultimate honeymoon for us, sweetheart."

"I'll never forget the look on your face the first time you saw the falls," said Leon, shifting gears as Miss Jibbie ground up a hill.

"The sheer magnificence of it boggled the mind," said Esther.

"The sound was incredible."

"The deep rumble of it crept inside everything. You could feel it in your bare feet in the hotel room."

"The sight of so much water going over the edge–awesome!" Leon threw in the clutch and coasted down the next hill.

"Yes, even looking out our window did not prepare you for the experience of walking closer and closer until you felt almost swept over the brink of eternity yourself," said Esther.

"Imagine going over the falls!"

"Terrifying!"

"Two sisters were rescued from the river above the falls while we were there. They had been staying in the campground." Leon slowed down while some chickens crossed the road. He joyfully beeped the horn –Ooo-ga. Half the chickens flapped their wings and hurried across the road. The other half turned around and ran back.

"No way would I ever go swimming in the Niagara river."

"I'll make you a bet, Leon. Can you name the first person to survive going over the falls in a barrel?"

"What prize do I win if I can name her?" asked Leon.

"Oh, you're sneaky. You know her, don't you?"

"Annie Edson Taylor in October 1901. You were just a baby. Now I will have my prize." He leaned over and puckered his lips, while keeping one eye on the road and one hand on the steering wheel.

Esther gave him a quick peck. "Leon, you aren't driving Gibraltar anymore. You need to pay attention when you are driving Miss Jibbie," she chided him a bit.

"Right you are, Babe, but I'm working on getting this new horse trained. She'll know the way home, soon," he chuckled.

"Leon, were you frightened at all, taking a ride in the 'Maid of the Mist?'"

"Who me?"

"Yes you. Now I demand the truth."

"Um, truth. Yes…well, I'll have to admit I was gripping onto those hand rails pretty tight."

"Leon, I was absolutely terrified. I still can't believe how close we came to the falls."

"They say the Maid of the Mist has one the most powerful maritime engines available. You didn't have doubts we would make it, did you?"

"On the contrary, I absolutely knew without a doubt we were headed for a certain death," said Esther.

Leon laughed and patted her legs. "No worries, Esther, your big strong knight in shining armor was right there holding you tight. Hey, it rhymes! Knight, right and tight." Leon burst into song,

"There once was a knight.

His pants were too tight.

He held you just right.

With muscles of might."

Esther groaned and tapped his arm, "You silly man. So why were you were holding on to me so tightly? It was hard to tell through the rubber suit," she teased.

"You caught me," Leon laughed.

"You know, I was scared walking behind the American falls, too."

"It was a weird feeling, wasn't it?"

"Yes and the steps down to it were slippery, weren't they? I was glad for the handrails," she said.

"I enjoyed the drive up and down the river, didn't you? The Queen Victoria Park was beautiful."

"The river was just as frightening as the falls but in a different sort of way." She stifled a yawn.

"Getting sleepy, darling?"

"I'll admit my nights have been disturbed somewhat by a certain person who shall remain nameless."

"I may be acquainted with the same person," chuckled Leon. "Why don't you lay your head down in my lap for a while?"

Esther lay down, closed her eyes and drifted off to sleep to the whining of the automobile wheels and the chuga-chuga-chug of the motor.

***

Six days later, dusty, tired but happy, Leon steered Miss Jibbie into their new driveway. Esther gazed at the house, stretched her back and did a three hundred sixty-degree turn. Except for a few scattered houses and buildings the horizon stretched away for miles in all directions, perfectly flat and almost treeless. "Well, we're here," she noted, feeling as flat as the view.

"Not a very exciting landscape is it, Esther, but we'll be just fine here. I know I'll be happy. I have a new job, a new life and most of all you."

She smiled at him, "Yes, we have each other and that's what counts."

"Come along dearest; let's look over our new place." He approached the front door, swept her up and carried her over the threshold. A tour of the rooms restored Esther's good humor. "I think this will do us nicely Leon, until we can afford to buy our own home."

"I know you can make this into a cozy home for us, Esther. And I will do my part, working as hard and as smart as I can at my new job so we can put away enough to buy a home of our own."

***

True to his word Leon worked diligently and honestly at his job driving a gas delivery truck. He was never late nor did he miss a day of work. There was no question but he missed the farm, the horse, cattle and other animals, the beautiful trees, lakes and hills of Michigan and the changing seasons. Yet, he kept his own counsel, never hinting to Esther of his homesickness.

Likewise Esther made the best of their situation. She faithfully wrote to Millie and Walter each week and lived for the arrival of letters from home. The days became weeks, the weeks soon turned into months and then years.

Little by little their bank account grew slowly but steadily. Esther took out the bank book and checked the balance from time to time. She had hoped they might be able to return to Michigan before they started their family, so she was not disappointed when she didn't conceive again for three years.

Christmastime 1922 came and went. Once more she and Leon were alone around their gaily decorated tree on Christmas Eve. They read the Christmas story, exchanged gifts and opened the boxes from home. They had made friends in Kansas, but those folks were all busy with their own families during the holidays.

January arrived amid snow blizzards and chilly winds. There were days when Leon was unable to drive out on his job. On those days he built up the fire and stayed close to the kitchen and Esther.

"I've been thinking, Esther."

"Oh-oh," she joked. "Does this mean I'm in trouble again?"

"One might say so. What I was thinking was to ask you how you would feel about trying for another baby?"

She turned away from the stove and sat down with him at the table. "Tell me about it," she said.

"Well, it has been what, three years since the baby? Is it time now, to start our family?"

"Well, I was hoping we could get back to Michigan first, but we've been here longer than either one of us expected. Business is good. I think we can afford a baby. You realize once I become pregnant, I won't be able to travel until the baby is old enough? We would be committing ourselves to at least one more year here. I've made friends here. It won't be the same as having my mother to deliver me, but I have you and my friends. Let's try and see what happens."

"You know, it isn't beyond the realm of possibility Millie could come out here. The trains are more comfortable than ever."

"Oh darling, can I write her right away?"

"Yes, let's ask her out next spring. What do you say?"

Esther clapped her hands in delight and did a little dance. Once again, her joy returned.

    ***

By springtime Esther was once again with child. The new family member was expected sometime in October, 1923.

When Millie arrived in April for a two-week visit, Esther was already over her morning sickness and blooming with health. The two of them had a marvelous time, once again preparing a layette for the baby, decorating and furnishing the nursery. Millie had been able to bring some of the more important baby items with her from Michigan.

Esther and Leon devoured the news from home. Walter was getting more gray hair but was still strong and healthy. They had hired one of the young men from town as Walter's new helper. Gibraltar was in his retirement, spending his days munching on clover and begetting a strong line of beautiful colts. Leon could have his choice when he returned to Michigan.

After a lengthy incarceration and trial, Otis had been sent away to an institution where he would get some help but would be confined for the rest of his life. The mayor and sheriff in town who had bungled the investigation were voted out of office. The gossip had died down.

Esther couldn't keep up with the two of them talking into late hours. She had to get to bed for the good of the baby and herself, as well. Every evening about nine-thirty she started to yawn and threatened to nod off in her rocking chair. "Goodnight, honey, see you tomorrow," she kissed Leon and then Millie and toddled off to bed.

On one of those late evenings, Millie told Leon in confidence of a rumor of a good farm coming on the market in Spring Arbor Township, east of Concord. "I can't promise, Leon, but it looks like a really good possibility. The elderly gentlemen who owns it hasn't been well. His wife is gone and they had no children.

"I've been doing what you asked before you left," continued Millie. "I've been keeping my feelers out for a good farm for you. One of my friends at church gave me a tip on this place. If the owner dies, it will go into his estate. Then there will be a six month's wait for probate before it will be auctioned.

"Sounds interesting," said Leon. "Tell me more,"

"Well, Walter has gone out to look the place over. He says there are two hundred tillable acres, a good-sized wood lot and plenty of water. The farm is on two sides of a good county road. A railroad track borders one side of the farm and a river the other side. There is a one room school house a half mile or so down the road and some close enough neighbors. It has two barns, outbuildings, a fresh water well and a new farm house with several bedrooms and all the latest improvements. The best part is the place would be just seven miles from our house."

"Millie, this sounds exactly like what I want. Let's not tell Esther, though. It's too soon to get her hopes up. I trust Walter's opinion even more than my own."

"But, how could you go about buying the place by long distance?"

"I will have papers drawn up before you leave, giving you power of attorney to act on my behalf in this deal. Also I'll draw you a bank draft you can use when you need it. Then, if the farm comes up for sale, I trust you and Walter to act on my behalf. Will you do it?"

182

"Of course I will, Leon. This is so exciting. We'll hope for the best. We may be able to approach the owner now and see whether he would entertain an offer on the place. What do you think?"

"Great idea! Perhaps we could purchase an option, or we could buy the place while giving him a lease to stay and work it until we can get out there. Use your judgment. We'll stay in touch."

"On another subject," he continued, "How was the train ride?"

"It was fun and not too tiring. Why do you ask?"

"Well, I've been thinking. You know, Esther believes she will be stuck here in Kansas until the baby is old enough to travel. I'm wondering what your opinion would be if I sent her home on the train, instead of by automobile. How soon could she travel?"

"Oh, it would be no problem at all. I saw plenty of pregnant ladies on the train and several small babies, too. We modern women are becoming quite adventuresome." Millie grinned. "Of course, Esther will have to stay close to home the last two months of her pregnancy, especially after what happened with Baby Girl, and she won't dare take the baby far for the first month. After that, train travel should be no problem. The train people are well prepared to assist. If Esther is successful nursing the baby, travel should be a snap, no food preparation problems."

"Okay, Millie, I'm convinced. Let's do it. Wouldn't it be perfect if we could be back in Michigan by this time next year, maybe sooner?"

"There is no one I know who deserves it more than you Leon. Well now, it is time for me to hit the hay," she kissed his cheek. "Pleasant dreams, Leon."

"Goodnight, Millie. You're the best." He patted her hand fondly.

***

EPILOGUE – Baptism

Leon took her arm and carefully helped his wife and new baby boy approach the altar. Esther had been safely delivered of a handsome, robust, eight-pound boy on October 11, 1923. Leon took the baby in his arms and stood beside his wife as the preacher read from the Order of Baptism of an Infant. He laid down the book of ceremonies and reached for the baby.

The infant boy turned his brown eyes toward the solemn-faced preacher and gazed in wonder. The pastor turned and took water in his hand, "And what name shall I give this child?" he inquired. Leon's voice was strong and proud. "His name is Leon Walter."

The Pastor intoned, "I baptize thee Leon Walter in the name of the Father, and of the Son and of the Holy Spirit." With each phrase he placed more handfuls of holy water on the tiny bald head. Walt scrunched up his little face and let out a startled cry. Every woman in the congregation sighed, "Aw." Every man chuckled. Little Walt continued screaming until Leon took him back into his arms and then handed him to his mother who began to bounce him and whisper sweet nothings to him as mothers have done for centuries.

Later, after the weary baby was fast asleep in his cradle, Esther and Leon sat on their porch enjoying a cup of tea. Leon couldn't keep the secret any longer, "Esther, I have a gift for you and Walt. It is a bit of a surprise. Would you like to open it, now?"

"A gift? For us? You didn't spend too much, did you?"

"Guilty," admitted Leon.

"Well, I never could stop you from overindulging me with gifts. Let's have it," sighed Esther in mock resignation.

"I'll give you two guesses. Part of it is small and part of it is very big."

"Some hint!" she scoffed. "Let me see. I shall need another hint."

"Oh, never mind, you'd never guess. Here, take these." He handed her two envelopes.

Esther tore the first one open and withdrew two tickets. "What is this?" she wondered. She scrutinized the printing on the tickets, "This constitutes one-way passage, Kansas City to Jackson – one adult passenger. This other one says one child under age six. One way? What is this for, Leon? Mother and Dad will love to see their grandson and I will love to see my parents, but why one way? Surely you want us to return."

Leon could barely contain his excitement. "Look inside the other envelope, Esther. There is something else."

She opened several sheets of paper and read, "Brown and Brown Realtors...The County of Jackson... Official deed... to a certain two hundred plus acres located in section four, the township of Spring Arbor... Oh dear God, Leon, what have you done?"

"It's ours, Esther. It's yours and mine, our new home, our farm. We are all going back to Michigan! Surprise!"

"But..." Esther was dumbfounded.

"It's true, darling."

"This is wonderful! But how could you inspect the farm or sign the papers, how did you know it was what you want? How did you do it?"

"Walter and Millie did everything for us, darling. We've been working on it ever since Millie's visit here last April. We've been writing back and forth for weeks."

"Oh my goodness! You sneaky man."

"You were busy growing little Walt. I didn't want to get your hopes up in case it fell through, and when it finally came together last week, I decided to surprise you after the baptism. We're going home, Esther! You and Walt on the train and I'll bring Miss Jibbie."

"Oh, Leon, you are so clever! This is fantastic! I'll have to pinch myself to make sure this isn't a dream."

"Are you pleased, Esther? Are you happy?"

"This is the second happiest day of my life, Leon. Thank you, thank you so much. I love you."

"I love you and Walt, too, both of my little ones." Leon took her in his arms. *"God is good! God is very good!"*

***

The End

Dear Reader,

If you enjoyed this book, we would be **ever so grateful** if you would go to the web page where you ordered it and leave a brief recommendation. Thank you so very much. Please go here: _www.amazon.com_ and search for Dorothy May Mercer in books. Or visit our website at MercerPublications.com for links to all of our books and booklets. For a 25% discount coupon on your next Mercer Publications title, please visit our web site. www.http://MercerPublications.com

In the United Kingdom, please go here: www.amazon.co.uk.

Leon and Esther can be found on all the amazon websites.

The Author and Publishers

References

"Put on Your Old Grey Bonnet', Words: Stanley Murphy. Music: Percy Wenrich. Pub.: Jerome H. Remick& Co., N.Y., 1909

"My Pony Boy" Interpolated into the show *Miss Innocence.* Words: Bobby Heath. Music: Charley O'Donnell. Pub. Jerome H. Remick & Co. N.Y., 1909

"Down by The Old Mill Stream" Words and Music: Tell Taylor. Pub: Tell Taylor Music Publisher, Chicago 1910

"Let Me Call You Sweetheart," Words: Beth Slater Whitson. Music Leo Friedman. Pub.: Harold Rossiter Music Company. Chicago 1910

Statistics on Niagara Falls from "Niagara Falls" by Rupert Brooke

www.ingramcontent.com/pod-product-compliance
Lightning Source LLC
Chambersburg PA
CBHW020957180626
46814CB00003B/1131